DATE DUE

FE 2 2 '06	JE 1 2 '08	
MR 0 3 '06	NOV 0 7 2010	
MR 1 4 '06		
MR.2 8 '06		
MY 1 1 06 06		
MY 3 0 '06		
JN 1 9 06		
AG 2 1 '06		
AG 2 8 '06		
OC 1 2 06		
OC 2 7 '06		
NO 2 9 '06		
DE 1 6 '06		
JA 2 3 07		
FE 2 1 07		

ROYAL BLUE

ROYAL BLUE

•

Kat Attalla

AVALON BOOKS

NEW YORK

F
Att

Published by Thomas Bouregy & Co., Inc.
160 Madison Avenue, New York, NY 10016

Library of Congress Cataloging-in-Publication Data

Attalla, Kat.
  Royal blue / Kat Attalla.
    p. cm.
  ISBN 0-8034-9753-9 (alk. paper)
  1. Advertising—Perfumes industry—Fiction. 2. Brooklyn (New
York, N.Y.)—Fiction. 3. Nobility—Fiction. I. Title.

  PS3551.T7218R69 2006
  813'.54—dc22

                                                    2005025394

PRINTED IN THE UNITED STATES OF AMERICA
ON ACID-FREE PAPER
BY HADDON CRAFTSMEN, BLOOMSBURG, PENNSYLVANIA

I dedicate this book to the wonderful nurses and talented doctors of the Hackensack University Medical Center, Stem Cell department. My special thanks to Dr. Goldberg and Phyllis—I wouldn't have made it without you.

I offer my special thanks to the truly talented women of the Tuesday Night critique group and the members of the Hudson Valley Romance Writers. And to my very first critique partners, Carol Butti and Susan Lock (a.k.a. my sisters).

Chapter One

To anyone else, today was just another Thursday but to Nick Lanborne it was one of the biggest days of his career. He pushed the manila folder to the side of the mahogany desk and glanced at the glossy photograph below. The raven haired beauty in the picture stared back at him. Long legs encased in black denim straddled the back of a Harley Davidson. The collar of her white shirt peeked out of a fitted leather jacket and windblown hair tumbled around her shoulders. She wasn't a fashion model, but she had that indefinable quality he was looking for. Sensual and wild. The kind of woman who would never be tamed and who was therefore irresistible to men.

The candid shot of the sultry woman even caused his stone heart to beat faster. Was this sexy waitress really the youngest of the Markova family?

He returned his attention to the report on his desk. A historian, a noted genealogist, and a private investigator all came to the same conclusion: Alexis Marks was the great granddaughter of Alexander Markova, the last ruling prince of Montavia before the communist unification of Eastern Europe. While the country no longer existed, the title fortunately still belonged to its descendants.

Tracing the family to America had been only half the battle. Now he needed to sign her onto the House of Yanis advertising campaign and turn the Brooklyn born wildcat into the royal princess she was.

"Good morning, Mr. Lanborne." Dolores Anderson, his administrative assistant, entered the office with a cup of coffee and the daily papers. "Or should I say, Your Highness?"

The comment from the poker faced matron had him choking on his coffee. "What?"

"The press is hailing you as the King of Madison Avenue. Must have something to do with that award you refuse to display."

Nick saw no point in flashing the small statue around the office. The financial success of the Avi-Star campaign meant more to him than the industry award he had received for the advertising project. Recognition, however, had its uses. It brought him the Costas account. Yanis Costas was a temperamental, but talented designer who was popular with the in crowd of socialites and nouveau riche. He was willing to pay a small fortune to make his new fragrance the toast of the fashion world.

"Did you get that number for me?" Nick asked.

"In your computer."

"Work or home number?"

"Work. I couldn't find a home number."

"Address?" he added.

"Listed below the number."

"The meeting with Costas . . ."

"Set for next Friday."

Nick chuckled. "What would I do without you?"

"Fold the company, at the very least, Your Highness."

Despite her droll tone, Nick was aware of just how much Dolores did for the company. She ran the office like a drill sergeant and still garnered the respect and admiration of her coworkers. Professionally, he couldn't survive without her. On a personal level, no woman would ever have that much power over him.

He had learned his work ethics from his workaholic father. His distrust of women came from his absent mother. Too bad he hadn't learned the second lesson well enough, as he'd repeated his father's mistakes in his own choice of a fiancé. With a shake of his head, he wiped the thought from his mind. It was ancient history.

Once he reviewed his agenda for the day and had the office to himself again, he picked up the phone to dial the number from the computer.

"Accounting. Talk to me." The informal greeting in a velvety smooth voice caught him by surprise.

He loosened the tie knotted at his throat. "Is this Alexis Marks?"

"Yes. Who is this?"

"Nick Lanborne of the Lanborne Agency."

"What can I do for you?"

Allow me to use your name and title to land the biggest account of the year. An account that used to belong to his ex-boss. Fair trade, Nick figured. He got the Costas account and his ex-boss got Nick's social-climbing former fiancé. All things considered, Nick got the better end of the deal. Clients paid the bills. Women were nothing but a big expense, both financially and emotionally.

"Are you there?" she asked.

"Yes. I'm sorry." He inhaled deeply. "Are you the granddaughter of Nadianna Marks?"

"Has something happened to my grandmother?" Her words echoed with panic. He should have realized it would be a natural assumption.

"No. Not at all. I'm just trying to make sure that I have the right Alexis Marks."

An awkward silence followed. He gripped the phone tighter. As first impressions go, he was making a lousy one.

"And which Alexis Marks are you looking for?" Her voice took on a noticeably skeptical tone.

Too late, he realized he should have had his first meeting with her in person. "Are you the great-granddaughter of Alexander Markova, Prince of Montavia."

Her annoyed grunt echoed in his ear. "Who put you up to this?"

"Excuse me?"

"Tell that loser, Tony, to get a life and leave me alone."

"You're mistaken . . ."

"No, you are. If you've got nothing better to do with your time, I suggest you try one of those nine hundred numbers. I'm sure you'll find a woman willing to amuse you for only ninety-five cents a minute."

A loud click was followed by silence. He stared at the receiver for several seconds before hanging up. Could it be that despite double-checking with immigration records and the Historical Society, he had the wrong woman? Many deposed royals had married money in return for their titles. Why had Nadianna Markova changed her name and settled as a commoner in Brighton Beach, Brooklyn? Granted, many Eastern European families emigrated there, but not the royalty. They had preferred Paris or Venice. Why hadn't the Markova family followed suit? He would have to check with the detective before trying again with the sultry-voiced woman.

Alexis sprinted from the subway station to the small brownstone where she lived with her grandmother. A quick glance at her watch told her she had five minutes to spare. She couldn't afford to pay the home health aid overtime again. With her two jobs, she was barely making ends meet.

"How is she today?" Alexis asked the woman who was waiting by the door as she entered.

"For the most part, she's lucid. She had a short spell earlier when we went out for a walk. She thought I was the nanny, taking her for a walk in the gardens."

The neighborhood of row houses didn't have a garden within ten miles of the place, unless she counted the window boxes. A hollow ache settled over her heart. Her grandmother's lapses in memory were getting more frequent and lasting longer.

She dropped her purse and keys on the small table by the door. "I'll take over now."

"Lexie. You really should consider an assisted living facility. She does have Social Security . . ."

"No thanks!" Alexis said with an angry wave of her hand. "I've already seen some of those state-run homes."

Her grandmother's condition was deteriorating daily. It was only a matter of time before her Nana would need more than the part time health aid that Alexis could barely afford now. She had checked into several public and private facilities. Most had been stark and frighteningly inadequate. She couldn't do that to the woman who had raised her and cared for her all these years. The only facility she had seen that she would consider cost three thousand dollars a month more than she could afford. Since Nana's retirement fund had gone to pay for Alexis' college, there were no savings to cover long term care.

"Oh, your landlord, Tony stopped by today.

Handsome guy," the young aid said with an admiring glint in her eye.

Alexis swallowed a groan. *Sure. If you like the macho, obnoxious type who thinks he's God's gift to the female population.*

During her early years, her family had been the joke of the neighborhood. "The Princesses of Brighton Beach," the neighbors had taunted her mother and grandmother. Alexis had been too young to remember much more than the regal way they handled the scorn. After her parents' death in a car accident fifteen years ago, the comments had ended. That was, until Tony had inherited the apartment building she lived in from his father and decided he wanted more than the rent from her each month. When she refused, he tried to get to her by reviving the taunting that had hurt her so much during childhood. The memory of her call this morning caused her anger to rise again. It looked as if her landlord was having his friends harass her at work.

Well, she wasn't a child, and she had learned how to shield her emotions against cruel words. Some people might even say she had a sharp tongue herself, she thought with a smile. But only the people who ticked her off.

She joined her grandmother at the kitchen

table. The once stylish woman no longer fixed her hair and barely dressed in more than her house coat. It broke Alexis' heart to see her this way. "Hi, Nana. How was your day?"

The older woman smiled. "Lexie."

"What would you like for dinner?"

"Tell the cook I'd love some borscht."

In the heat of the summer, Alexis wasn't about to cook soup, even if she knew the recipe, which of course, she didn't. Nor could she afford the luxury of a cook. Lately her grandmother's strange requests made Alexis wonder how much of Nana's ramblings about servants and palaces were fantasy and how much were memory.

An hour later, while she cleaned up after a light dinner of sandwiches and salad, she still pondered the question. The taunts she remembered from childhood must have come from somewhere. Could her Nana really be . . . ? *Get real, Alexis.* Why would a bonafide royal princess have settled in Brooklyn and taken a factory job? Her grandmother never talked about her life before coming to America. At least not to Alexis.

A knock on the front door put an end to her curious musing. She scooted across the living room floor and looked through the security peek hole at the man standing outside her apartment. Even with the distortion caused by the concave lens, he had an imposing presence. He wore what appeared to be an expensive suit, although she knew little about high-end fashions. A briefcase under his arm, he paced the threadbare carpet in the hall.

She opened the door slightly, keeping her foot wedged firmly behind it. What she couldn't see though the peephole now stared her straight in the face. An arresting pair of deep green eyes that sparkled so clearly she wondered if the color was real or the result of designer lenses. The spicy scent of aftershave tickled her nostrils and tingled her nerve endings.

"Alexis Marks?" His voice played over her ears like a country western ballad. Soulful, sexy, with a hint of arrogance.

She must be working too many hours, she thought, if some stranger in a fancy suit could cause her heart to flutter and her knees to go weak. At twenty-five she was too young for hot flashes and too old for schoolgirl crushes. And, by now, she was too smart to believe that Mr. Wonderful would be delivered to her door like a Domino's Pizza.

"Are you Alexis Marks?" he asked again.

"Who's asking?"

"Nick Lanborne. We spoke earlier."

After an initial moment of confusion, the name and earlier conversation came back to her. She felt as if she'd been broadsided. Before she could slam the door in his face, Nick Lanborne stuck his expensive loafer inside.

"Get lost," she snapped.

"I just want to speak to you."

She wrestled with the door to no avail. His strength was greater than hers. "This joke is getting very old."

His gaze captured hers. There was no humor in his expression. "All I want is ten minutes of your time. If you still think it's a joke, I'll leave."

Despite his calmly spoken words she sensed his frustration. He was persistent and determined. She doubted he would go so far for a mere joke. "Even if you aren't joking, I think you have the wrong woman."

"I don't."

Nick Lanborne apparently wasn't going to leave until he had his say and she had neither the patience nor the desire to continue the argument in the hall where any of her nosey neighbors would overhear. "Ten minutes."

He nodded and stepped into her small living room. She left the front door open. Nana had already retired, and luckily she was a sound sleeper. Lexie didn't want to cause her grandmother any embarrassment or hurt over something that was a case of mistaken identity at best, or something far more cruel. Pushing a crocheted afghan aside, she offered Nick a seat on the sofa.

"Clock's ticking," she said the minute he sat down.

He placed his briefcase on the coffee table in front of him. With a flip of the locks, he opened the top and removed some papers. "I'd like you to take a look at this."

"Okay. I'll play along," she muttered.

She sat in an old recliner and glanced through the folder he handed her. It contained an array of papers, including documents of immigration, photographs and old newspaper clippings of the royal family before the fall of Montavia. The names and places sounded completely alien, except for one; the young Princess Nadianna Markova standing next to her father, the crown prince. Also included were reports from some genealogical society that claimed her grandmother was the daughter of the last ruling prince of Montavia. Very official looking documents that could be entirely fake.

"And, your point?" she asked, wondering what his angle was in finding her.

"Excuse me?"

"Even if this was true, which I doubt, what is it you want from me, Mr. Lanborne?" She tossed the folder onto the coffee table and rose from the chair. "I mean, look at me. Do I look like some lost princess to you?"

He shifted in his seat. His eyes narrowed in anger, but he seemed to keep a lid on his temper. He apparently wasn't used to having his word questioned. "I assure you, it's real. I've had it verified by a historian and two separate genealogists."

She slid her hands into the pockets of her worn jeans. "Well, you've certainly been thorough."

"I needed to be absolutely sure."

Even if she could believe the proof before her—and she was still skeptical about its authenticity—what did it mean to her or her grandmother now? The country of Montavia no longer existed. She doubted there were some fabulously expensive crown jewels waiting to be claimed. Nick Lanborne had gone to an enormous effort and expense to research a worthless piece of history. He must have expected something as a return on his investment. "So, I repeat, Mr. Lanborne. What is it you want from me?"

Nick glanced around the apartment rather

than meet her scrutinizing gaze. The furniture had seen better days, but the small room was tidy and had a cozy feel. A window fan circulated humid air around the room, but did little else to relieve the oppressive summer heat. He loosened his tie and collar.

His gaze returned to Alexis. She was dressed in a pair of shorts and a sleeveless cotton top, with her long hair piled on top of her head. The photograph hadn't done her justice. Her eyes were bluer, her lips fuller, her curves more rounded. Everything about her was more than he had expected. Including her skepticism. He figured he would be talking money by this point. Instead he was still trying to convince her he wasn't some con man looking to sell her swampland. However, seeing her in person only convinced him that he wanted her . . . for the advertising campaign.

He couldn't afford to see her as anything more than a commodity. She had some rough edges that needed to be smoothed but with professional coaching and the right makeup and clothes, Princess Alexis could be the darling of New York's fashion elite.

"You haven't answered my question, Mr. Lanborne."

"Nick. And for now, I just want to convince you that this information is true."

"Why?"

Although he was a proud cynic himself, he wasn't used to being poised on the other side of the equation. He had built his reputation with straightforward business dealings and his word was rarely challenged. "Because what I want is immaterial if you don't believe what I'm saying."

"Don't you think I would know if I had a princess or two climbing around in my family tree?"

He had to admit, he couldn't figure that one out. Why had Nadianna Markova not told her granddaughter about her family heritage? "Then allow me to speak with your grandmother."

Her eyes glazed over in anger. "My grandmother is a sweet and trusting woman. You could probably convince her that I am the Queen of Sheba but it wouldn't make it true."

"Just a few questions . . ."

"No," she said. The tone of her voice was as cold as her ice blue stare. He admired her devotion, but it wasn't helping his cause. "If that's all, your ten minutes are up."

Nick clenched his fingers into fists. She was testing his patience and so far he was failing miserably. The woman was more trouble than she was worth . . .

No, she was worth the biggest account of

his career. He had already sold the client on the idea of the campaign and he needed to have her signed on by the end of the week if he was to close the deal.

"Tell me what it will take, Miss Marks."

She folded her arms across her chest. "Perhaps if I knew the point to all this, I might be more convinced."

"What do you mean?"

"I'm not stupid. You didn't go to all this trouble for my benefit. There has to be something in it for you."

Did she have to make him sound so Machiavellian? What he wanted would benefit her too. Her opinion of him shouldn't matter, but for some reason, it did. "Yes, there is something in it for me. And for you as well."

"Unless you are talking big bucks for something that isn't illegal, immoral, or indecent, I need to get some sleep. I have work tomorrow."

The irony of her offhanded wisecrack wasn't lost on him. She had no idea what that title she readily dismissed was worth. He collected his briefcase and came to his feet. His best plan was to leave her with something to sleep on. If she was like most women, she would jump at the opportunity he was presenting her. Before joining her at the door opened wide for his exit, he scribbled a note on the back of his business card.

"Your papers," she reminded him.

"You keep them. Read them over. Then give me a call." He took her hand and pressed the card into her soft fingers. The touch was brief, but the jolt to his system was immediate and completely unexpected. Judging by her widening eyes, she felt it too. Static electricity, he told himself. And he would have believed it if not for the kick of desire that followed. An attraction was not part of his carefully orchestrated plan. "Good night, Miss Marks."

Although she didn't say anything, her expression spoke volumes. She looked like he felt: confused and wanting no part of the attraction.

Chapter Two

Friday night, Alexis sat in the corner booth and picked at her dinner before the start of her shift. She had already put in an eight-hour day at the office where she worked as an accountant and she was dead tired. With only enough time to change into her western shirt and cowboy boots—required attire for her waitressing job at the country western steak house and saloon—she had run out the door again and hopped on the subway to the bar. Thankfully, Nana's bridge partner kept her company until she slept, but Lexie couldn't depend on the older woman's generosity forever. Friday night at the Silver Spur didn't pick up for another hour and usually ran till well past two in the morning. How was she going to make it though the night?

To say that her meeting with Nick Lanborne last evening had cost her a sleepless night was an understatement. At first she had refused to accept that the information he presented was authentic. Then she began looking for reasons to believe. Like the fact that her mother and grandmother had both kept their maiden name after marriage, or at least the anglicized version of it. Were they hoping to leave a trace of the family? And what about those fairy tales Nana used to tell her about a fantastic, far-off land and a young princess? The details had been so vivid that Alexis had often imagined herself riding a gilded, horse-drawn carriage around the snow covered grounds of a marble palace.

Her curiosity got the better of her, as Nick probably knew it would, and she did some checking on the genealogist and the historian who wrote the reports. Both were very well respected in their fields. Still, Alexis felt uneasy. If something seemed too good to be true, it probably was.

She turned over the business card he had given her and read the back again. The words had not disappeared. *Five hundred thousand dollars for two years of your time. Nothing*

illegal, immoral, or indecent. Well, what else
was worth half a million dollars? A man as
blatantly sexy as Nick Lanborne wouldn't
need to pay for female company. Nor did he
seem shallow enough to need to consort with
royalty to bolster his ego. So what did he want
from her that would pay so much money?

"What's this?" Marissa, fellow waitress and
her best friend, snapped the card from her
hand as she dropped into the bench across
from Alexis. "Who is Nick Lanborne?"

"I haven't a clue," she said. What did she
know about the sexy stranger who had visited
her last evening? Nothing. He had left before
she got a straight answer from him. Of course,
she had been too busy recovering from the
premature hot flashes he had inspired in her
body. It had been more than a year since she
had been on a date and even longer since she
had been so overwhelmingly attracted to a
man.

Marissa let out a long whistle. "Holy gua-
camole, Batgirl. This is some serious dinero.
What the heck would you have to do for that?
And for two straight years?"

"Beats me."

"Let's hope not," Marissa said with a laugh.
"It wouldn't be worth the money."

Alexis smiled for the fist time all week. "You are twisted."

"Hey, I'm not the one who was propositioned here. Is this for real?"

Alexis took the card back and slid it into the pocket of her Levi's. "I'm not sure."

"Okay, Lexie. Spill it. What's going on?"

Marissa had been her closest friend since their troublemaking adolescence at St. Mary's Girl Academy. She knew more about Alexis than any other person. In the past year, she had given up many nights to stay in with Alexis and her grandmother when she could have been out having a good time like other single twenty-somethings. But how could she begin to explain what was going on, even to her best friend? She wasn't sure she believed it herself. Or, she wasn't sure if she wanted to. She relayed the events of her meeting with Nick Lanborne, while leaving out her strange attraction to him. That was something she didn't want to dwell on. And something her friend would undoubtedly harp on for the rest of the night.

Marissa snapped her gum as she listened. She was aware of childhood taunts and Nana's strange comments of late, so she readily accepted the information gathered by Nick Lanborne. "So, what does he want?"

"I don't know."

"You are going to call him and find out, aren't you?"

"I'm still thinking about it."

"Are you outta your flippin' mind?" Marissa's words pitched, gaining the attention of the few patrons in the bar. She leaned in closer and lowered her voice. "What's to think about?"

"Assuming what he says is true about Nana, then there must be a reason she kept it a secret all these years. I also have to assume that Nick Lanborne wants to exploit the family name in some way or our family history wouldn't be an issue."

Marissa laid a comforting hand on her arm. "You can also assume that half a million dollars will pay for the best nursing care the Riverdale Nursing Home has to offer. Nana won't know. And face it, Lexie, it has to be better than spending her remaining days in a hot apartment with a home health aid."

She knew her friend was right. Those very same points had kept her up all night and sidetracked her half of the day. Before she could make any kind of decision, she would have to contact Mr. Lanborne and find out just what he wanted her to do in return for the money. Then she would have to decide if she could sell out her grandmother's past to ensure her future.

It had been a long, hot August weekend, Nick thought, and it seemed as if things would get even hotter now. By Monday afternoon, when he hadn't heard from Alexis, he figured she had written him off as a con artist. He didn't blame her. He'd even admired her courage for thumbing her nose up at the money, despite how important she was to landing the account. So her call Tuesday morning was both a relief and a disappointment. Not that he was disillusioned. She had lived up to his expectations. Money talked and a half a million dollars bought a heck of a lot of conversation.

He glanced at his watch. Almost noon. The lovely Alexis Marks was due at any moment. Anticipation caused his adrenaline to flow. The thrill of the deal, he told himself because he refused to admit to anything more. He slid her photograph back into the file on his desk at the same moment his assistant announced her arrival. Punctual. Well, at least she didn't have a princess mentality yet.

When she walked into the office he was forced to do a double take. Dressed in a simple brown skirt and cream colored silk blouse, he saw another facet of the woman he wanted to keep two dimensional in his mind. He wouldn't call her demure, with her wild expressive eyes and full mouth, but she looked more conservative than at his last meeting with her.

"Would you care to go to lunch?" he asked before she sat down.

"Not really. I only have a half hour. I'm due back at the office at one o'clock."

He offered her a chair and waited until she sat before taking the seat behind his desk. "If our negotiations go well, you won't need to go back."

She crossed her shapely legs at the ankles. He tried not to notice the hint of her smooth thigh exposed where her skirt had hiked up slightly. He suddenly felt flush. Had the air conditioning stopped working? "I don't know what it is you want, so negotiations might amount to nothing. And even if we do reach an agreement, I would still have to return to work and give two weeks notice."

A woman who honored her commitments. Now that was a rare thing indeed. His admiration for her hitched up a notch. "You have no idea what I want?"

She shrugged. "Your office is on Madison Avenue, so I thought it might have something to do with advertising, but I try not to make assumptions based on appearances." Was there a hint of reproach in her voice?

"Yes it has something to do with advertising. My client is interested in an exclusive licensing agreement with you."

Confusion caused her tweezed eyebrows to arch slightly. "Licensing what?"

"Your title and your likeness."

"I'm not following you." She shook her head. Dark waves of hair brushed her shoulders. The kind of thick, lustrous hair he wanted to bury his face in.

Whoa, he needed to bury these erotic thoughts.

"In other words, Princess Alexis Markova would be the spokesperson for Royal Blue, a new fragrance from the House of Yanis."

A breath seemed to catch in her throat. Her eyes rounded. "You're kidding, right?"

"You are familiar with the designer Yanis Costas?"

"Who isn't? And he'll pay five hundred thousand dollars to use my name and picture?" Her voice pitched as if she thought he was crazy.

"I said it wasn't illegal, immoral, or indecent. I didn't say it would be that easy. It's not as if he wants to stick a crown on your head and snap a photograph."

She regarded him for a long, silent moment. Her scrutiny unsettled him. Blatant appraisal was nothing new to him, but he got the feeling she was sizing up more than his looks. She was assessing his character as well.

"Precisely what is your client after?" she finally asked.

"He wants a princess and by the time he's done with you, that is exactly what you will be. Everything about you will be changed, from your style of hair, the clothes you wear, even where you live. For the next two years, the only thing you'll be able to control are your thoughts."

Was he trying to sabotage his own ad campaign? Nick didn't want to glamorize the offer, but he didn't need to make it sound so oppressive either.

"Sounds like a stint in the army," she muttered.

"I suppose you could look at it that way."

"Except the pay is better," she noted a small smile.

"Considerably."

She paused as if giving the matter thought. Conflicting emotions played across her face. "What about my personal life, Mr. Lanborne?"

"What do you mean?"

Alexis leaned in closer, capturing his gaze.

"Do I have to answer to the client for my private life as well?"

The thought of her having a "private life" with some man caused an ache in his gut, but he had no idea why. He couldn't very well ask if she was involved in a serious relationship, through he wanted to. Not that it affected the deal one way or another, but his own sense of curiosity was strangely unsatisfied. "Of course not. We *would* ask that you be discrete since you will be in the spotlight, but hey, you wouldn't be the first royal to have your life splashed across the tabloids."

"I'm not a royal, in that sense of the word."

"Oh, but you are, Alexis Markova." She winced at his use of her true name.

Obviously uncomfortable, she rose and walked around the office. His gaze followed her as she circled the office. He had lucked out. Her natural grace was something that couldn't be taught. The rest was window dressing.

"I have to be getting back to work," she said.

"You haven't told me if you plan to sign on."

"I'm not sure yet."

"Why don't you take a copy of the contract. Have your lawyer check it over, and get back to me."

"All right," she said as she took the paper

from his hand. "I'll call you in a couple of days."

He was reluctant to let her escape so soon, and for that reason alone he didn't try to stop her. If things went as planned, they would be spending more time with each other in the next few months than many married couples. He needed to get his hormones in check and keep a professional distance.

A few moments later, Dolores knocked on his office door. "Did she sign on?"

He glanced at the unsigned papers on his desk. "Not yet, but she will."

"You seem very sure," his office manager said.

As sure as he could be without the actual signature on the contract. Alexis Marks might be wrestling with her conscience now but he felt certain she would take the cash in the end. Women always did.

Alexis sat at the kitchen table in the small, hot apartment. She pushed back a strand of damp hair that clung to her cheek in the oppressive heat. What she wouldn't give for air-conditioning. Since her landlord refused to allow an electrician to update the wiring, she blew a circuit when ever she tried to run the old unit. Several calls to various city agencies had yet to yield any results.

She recalled her earlier meeting with Nick Lanborne. She wasn't sure what to make of the man. First he had offered her a fantastic deal, then he had tried to scare her off the project. Why? If Yanis Costas was willing to pay her so much money, it stood to reason that Nick would make even more for the overall campaign.

He was a mystery—aloof and self-contained. Not at all the kind of man she was usually attracted to. So why couldn't she banish the image of the gorgeous, green-eyed man from her thoughts? She had a big decision to make, one that would affect her entire life. Nick Lanborne was the last person to take into account when she made up her mind. Even her own misgivings took second place to what was best for her grandmother.

Several times at dinner she had started to ask her grandmother about her life before coming to America, but she couldn't do it. From what she'd read in the reports, Nana had suffered tragic losses in her youth. Then, to bury her own child and raise her granddaughter couldn't have been easy.

Now Alexis had it in her power to make her grandmother's remaining days comfortable and happy. Two years wasn't that long of a sentence in return for the lifetime of devotion and support Nana had given her. She wasn't being asked to endure hard labor. However, nothing in life was free.

Everything about you will be changed, from your style of hair, the clothes you wear, even where you live. For the next two years, the only thing you'll be able to control are your thoughts.

Could she really let someone have that much control over her life? As she listened to the nightly newscaster talk about the toll the heat and ozone conditions took on the elderly, she knew she didn't have much choice.

Chapter Three

Three days later in Nick Lanborne's office once again, Alexis got her first taste of what her life was about to become. Yanis Costas, the flamboyant and talented designer, was nothing like she expected. The man had striking features that were more beautiful than handsome. With his Greek-American heritage he could pass for Adonis himself. He wore tailored clothes that draped perfectly on his well-toned body. His hair was impeccably styled and manicured hands waved enthusiastically as he spoke.

He spent the first hour discussing the considerable number of her flaws that would have to be overcome. Her skin was too pale, her hair had no shape or style and her taste in clothes . . . well, she got the impression he thought she shopped at the Salvation Army. What the heck did the man want with an obvious hag like her?

Through it all, Nick just sat there nodding in agreement and jotting notes on a legal pad. Several times, she wanted to tell both men where they could go and storm out of the office. And she would have if not for the fact that she had a late afternoon appointment with the financial department at the Riverdale Assisted Living Center. After a long internal struggle, Lexie had come to the heartbreaking conclusion that the modern, air-conditioned facility was better than round-the-clock nursing in their tiny, sweltering apartment. The Riverdale administrator wanted proof that Alexis could make the payments before her grandmother could be accepted in residence. Until she agreed to all the terms and signed the contract, she had to sit tight and keep her mouth shut.

"Ah, but she has such potential," Yanis finally announced. "She will do marvelously."

Nick shot a glance toward her. "Anything you wanted to ask, Princess?"

"Aside from the request that you don't call me Princess unless you plan to genuflect in my presence?" she quipped before she could stop herself. Being discussed by the two men as if she was a thing rather than a person had rankled her.

"I like her spirit," Yanis said with a booming chuckle that echoed around the room. "But that accent . . ."

Coming from a man whose own speech was as kaleidoscopic as his mannerisms, she had to hold back a laugh. Apparently, even her voice would have to be changed. What was next?

"All right, *Miss Markova*," Nick said. "Any questions?"

"It's Marks," she corrected.

"Not when you legally change it back to your original family name." He made it sound as easy as changing her clothes or her hairstyle. Maybe it was, in theory. He had obviously researched every angle thoroughly. Except the emotional angle.

Her stomach clenched into a tight knot. Was any amount of money worth losing her identity?

"You said my address would be changing too. Where will I be living?"

"Most of the time you will be staying in a company owned apartment that Mr. Costas had provided . . ."

"Please, you must both call me Yanis. By the time this is over, I will have left my mark over every inch of her. We should at least be on a first name basis."

A flash of anger sparked in Nick's eyes. His fingers gripped the end of the desk. If she didn't know better, it would seem to be the look of a jealous man.

"You said, *most of the time*."

He collected himself quickly. "During the launch of the ad campaign, which will coincide with the fall fashion shows in New York, you will occupy a suite at the Plaza. And, of course, you will be present for the shows in Paris and Milan."

"Of course," she repeated with a small gasp of surprise. Paris, Milan, New York. Would she be able to pull off what they wanted without feeling like a fraud? Even her lawyer had advised her to take the deal.

"So, are you on board, Princess?" Yanis asked. His welcoming expression was more embracing than Nick's frown.

What did he want? What did he expect? He had come to her, offered her the chance of a lifetime and now seemed to sit in judgment of her. She wished to God the money wasn't so important.

She closed her eyes and pictured Nana enjoying the comfort and care of Riverdale. "Yes," she forced out even as her heart cried no.

Nick collected the contracts to be sent to the lawyer and slid them into his briefcase. He stole a glance at Alexis as she spoke quietly with her new boss. For a woman who had just signed a sweetheart deal and held the first payment in her hand, she didn't seem happy. Was she sorry she hadn't held out for more money?

For a man who had just signed the biggest account of his career, he wasn't too thrilled himself. Where was that adrenaline rush he had expected? He should be ready to go out and celebrate.

Yanis whispered something to Alexis that made her smile. A sensual smile that could break hearts and wrap men around her slender finger. A smile that would be his downfall if he allowed himself to fall for her considerable charm.

"You were right, Nick. She is exquisite," Yanis said.

"You said that?" Alexis asked Nick in surprise. Her blue eyes widened.

"I don't know if they were my exact words," he grumbled. Then he cursed himself for revealing a personal opinion to his client. "If I did, I was speaking in aesthetic terms."

There was that smile again, only this time she was staring directly at him. Her eyes were as engaging as her enigmatic grin. "Of course. I wouldn't dare assume that you would pay me a personal compliment, Mr. Lanborne."

He wanted to pay her some *personal* attention though.

"My, but the three of us are going to have such fun," Yanis said with a dramatic wave of his hand. "I can hardly contain my excitement."

Nick had to put a lid on his own. Maybe that adrenaline was kicking in after all.

Once Yanis Costas left, an awkward silence settled between the two of them. He supposed he should take her to dinner, but she made him hungry for more than food. With their current business arrangement, that hunger would not be sated. He did have some class, however, despite his ex-fiancé's assertion that it wasn't high enough for her expensive tastes. A dinner with a professional associate in a crowded restaurant was harmless.

"Are you almost done scowling?" she asked. "I'm beginning to think you don't find me exquisite at all. It looks more like I'm giving you indigestion."

He shook his head. "You should learn not to

be so blunt. Diplomacy is a virtue of the aristocracy."

"I don't answer to you for two more weeks. Until then, I plan to revel in my tasteless middle-class style and spout undiplomatic observations in my Brooklyn accent." Her eyes reflected the hurt that her light comment was obviously meant to deny.

By seeking to change everything about her, he insulted the woman she was. And as far as he could tell, there was nothing wrong with the woman she was. Still, she knew the score before she decided to enter the game. Advertising was the art of illusion. He needed to sell the fantasy and that required a special look.

"Shall we discuss the campaign over dinner?"

"I can't. I have an appointment."

Why was he disappointed? "Another time, then."

"Sure." She collected her purse and looped the strap over her shoulder. Nervously, she fidgeted with the clasp. "I do have a question."

He nodded.

"What happens if I don't pull this off?"

She talked tough with words and still managed to project the perfect mix of vulnerability and fear in her voice. There wasn't anything

for her to pull off. She *was* Princess Alexis
Markova. She might not believe that yet, but
he had no doubt. "You will."

Two weeks later, Alexis sat with Marissa in
Sawbuck's enjoying a moccaccino, her one
concession to her new economic status.
Having had the pleasure of telling her harass-
ing landlord where to go that morning, she
was out celebrating . . . and drowning her sor-
rows. Although Nana had been moved into her
new residency at Riverdale without so much as
a single complaint, Alexis had felt a pang of
separation she hadn't counted on. Twenty-five
years in the same house with the same caring
person, was a lot to let go of.

"If you're not going to enjoy this, Lexie, we
should just leave," Marissa said. "There are
too many yuppies here for comfort."

"I can't leave. Mr. Lanborne is meeting me
here to give me the keys to my new apartment.
You go ahead, though, I'll be fine."

"Not until I meet this guy. Not for nothing,
Lexie, but if some joker takes over my best
friend's life, you better believe I'm gonna
check him out."

Which was precisely what Alexis wanted to
avoid. If her friend wasn't all over the man
herself in five minutes, she would be trying to

convince Alexis to mix business with pleasure. Despite Marissa's feigned distaste of yuppies, she still considered the successful business-man the American equivalent of Prince Charming. Trade the white steed for a black BMW and the shining armor for an Armani suit, but the principle was the same.

"How come you never talk about him?"

"What's to talk about?" Should she tell her friend how she had daydreams about a man who saw her as a commodity? It was disheart-ening to think that he would probably have the same emotions for a box of cereal if a client was asking him to deliver a campaign.

"On a scale of one to ten?" Marissa pushed.

"I didn't notice," Alexis lied.

"That bad?"

That good. There weren't enough numbers on the scale to rate him.

A few moments later, Nick entered the cof-fee shop and sauntered toward her. Female heads turned to watch him move. He had the same lazy grace as a lion and was probably every bit the predator when going after what he wanted.

"Are you finished here?" he asked.

"Not yet, but you're welcome to join us," Marissa purred. Apparently thinking he was waiting for a table, she removed her purse from the chair next to her. A sexy pout and a sultry smile, her friend's ambush gear, were ready to engage the opponent.

"I think he means me." Alexis shrugged. "Mr. Lanborne, Marissa DeMartini."

"Nick," he said, offering his hand.

By Marissa's shocked gape, Alexis figured her friend was expecting Quasimoto's uglier brother. "Lexie, when was the last time you had an eye exam?"

"Don't you have to be back at work soon?" She hated to admit it, but she resented her friend's overt appraisal of Nick. Jealousy was a useless emotion that she had never wasted time with before. She especially felt bad because she was experiencing this "wasted emotion" toward a friend who had been giving and caring to both her and her grandmother. "Or maybe you can take the rest of the afternoon off and see the apartment with me. Unless that's a problem, Nick."

He met her questioning gaze but said nothing. Was he angry? He would make a great poker player. His expressions were so deadpan, so completely unreadable, that she couldn't begin to guess what went on in his mind. "Shall we go, ladies?"

"I can't," Marissa said. She leaned in closer to Alexis and whispered, "Your territory is marked and duly noted. Give me a call and I'll meet you there tonight."

She nodded, feeling guilty even though her friend didn't seem upset. In fact, Marissa looked quite amused.

"I need to make a quick run to the bathroom," Alexis said.

"I'll keep Mr. Lanborne company until you return."

Nick grinned.

Knowing her friend the way she did, Alexis almost felt sorry for him. He had no idea what was coming. If Marissa wasn't making a move, she was making a point. And she *always* got her point across.

Nick waited by the car for Alexis to finish her trip to the ladies' room. Her friend's parting warning still rang in his ear. The candid Miss DeMartini was not shy to tell him exactly what she would do if he or Costas did anything to hurt Alexis in any way. He admired the sentiment, if not the threat. He also couldn't stop himself from wondering about the woman who inspired such fierce loyalty from her friend. Alexis didn't come across as a person who needed defending. She knew how to take care of herself, and that job had just become financially easier.

Moments later, she joined him on the street. She was dressed in a pair of soft, faded jeans and a sleeveless shirt. The simple outfit surprised him. Considering how much money she had been paid up-front, he figured by now she would be decked out in a designer wardrobe replete with matching accessories. She'd had two weeks. Most women made a sport out of shopping.

Although Alexis' clothes for all public engagements would be supplied by the House of Yanis, he figured she would indulge herself in her personal needs. She wasn't what he expected. Her casual style was an expression of a woman who was comfortable with her life. Transforming her into an eloquent, sophisticated princess was going to be a more difficult undertaking when she clearly didn't want to be transformed. So why had she accepted the deal?

"Where's Marissa?" Alexis asked.

"She took off on her Harley."

"Oh. Sorry I kept you waiting."

He nodded.

"You must be very busy. You don't have to drive me. I'm sure I can find the address myself."

He rolled his shoulders in a casual shrug. "It's no big deal."

"Then try smiling or take an antacid for that persistent indigestion of yours." Her impish grin caused him to chuckle in spite of himself.

"You are a piece of work."

And a work of art. There were few women who could make him laugh, fewer still who roused his interest. But Alexis was the only one who accomplished both at the same time.

She tried to look contrite, but didn't pull it off. "Forgive me. I'm supposed to be more diplomatic."

He opened the car door for her. "Or remember that silence is a virtue."

"Silence was never my strongest suit," she said as she slid into the bucket seat.

"I gathered that." She was a woman who spoke her mind. A trait he greatly admired in her. Except when she decided to turn her potent charm in his direction.

He was going to have his hands full trying to keep his hands to himself. As a client, she was off limits, and there was nothing more enticing than something he couldn't have. The woman was a fascinating paradox. If she could just project for the camera that flirtatious innocence, that tender toughness, the campaign would succeed beyond his original expectation.

Why wasn't he pleased?

Because those very qualities that made her the perfect candidate for the position also made her irresistible to him. Rather than share her with the world, he wanted her to himself— a dangerous aspiration both professionally and personally. In the past few years he'd had no trouble putting work ahead of his personal life. Now was not the time to take a step backward.

Alexis moved through the ultra-contemporary apartment carefully, afraid she might break something. Her gaze darted around the rooms. The style was posh, designed to impress. The leather furniture was accented with brass and oriental lacquered pieces. Modern art in contemporary frames adorned the walls. Although she tried not to be impressed, the sheer beauty of it took her breath away. Would she ever feel like she belonged here?

The location, just south of Rockefeller Center and east of the theater district, was one of the most desirable and expensive areas of the city. With the Costas showroom one floor below, it was ideal for when she had to go for fittings as well as hair and makeup sessions. It was also convenient to reach the Riverdale Home for visits to her grandmother.

"What do you think?" Nick asked.

She turned to find him filling the archway between the living room and kitchen. The musky scent of aftershave pricked at her nerve endings. Her stomach fluttered. The man was too tempting for his own good . . . or hers. "It's beautiful. I suppose you'll want me to sign some sort of inventory sheet regarding the contents."

His eyes sparked. "If I was worried about you hocking the furniture, I wouldn't have signed you onto the account. Your former boss praised your honesty and integrity. I see no reason to question it."

She smiled and shook her head at the same time. "I think that was a compliment. So why are you mad at me?"

"I'm not."

Something was bothering him. Was he angry that she expected distrust from him? Did he really care what she thought about him? He would probably make a quick exit if he knew that his very nearness caused a heat wave in her. The way he looked at her, studied her, made her pulse race. She had received a fair amount of offers when she worked at the bar, but none that had sparked her interest.

Nick definitely lit a fire and she was flying too close to the flame. Curiosity was a danger-ous thing, especially when directed toward a man who clearly planned to keep her at a distance. So, what would it take to get a reaction from him? This was their fourth meeting and she knew nothing about him. But she wanted to. Too bad she wasn't privy to a dossier on him like the one he had collected on her.

"Do you need a second set of keys?" His question caught her by surprise.

"For what?"

"Will you be living alone?"

"Of course. My grandmother has moved to . . ." She didn't finish the sentence. His obvious expression of relief told her Nana wasn't who he was referring to. "Is that your roundabout way of asking if I have a man in my life?"

"It's not my business," he grumbled.

"But you want to know." The idea made her giddy. She'd been convinced her attraction was one-sided. Maybe not. But why did he go to such lengths to appear indifferent?

"It has nothing to do with our arrangement."

Something about Nick touched her in a way she couldn't understand. What made him different from all the other men she had met in her lifetime? She didn't know. The only thing she did know for certain was that she was drawn to him.

She crossed the room and stood in front of

him. "Admit it, Nick. You want to know." She stroked her hand over the soft lapel of his jacket. "Come on. Say it."

"All right. I want to know. For business . . ."

She pressed a finger to his warm lips. "Don't blow it with a lie. If you had business reasons for wanting to know, you would have investigated my personal life, not just my family history."

He caught her wrist in a steel grip. "Alexis." His voice held a trace of warning.

"That's the first time you've called me by my name." She liked the sound of it rolling over his tongue.

He wouldn't meet her gaze. "If we are going to be working together . . ."

Perhaps it wasn't wise to mix business with pleasure, but nothing was ever gained by playing it safe. If she didn't get this out of her system now, she would never be able to trust what she felt.

Beginning tomorrow, her appearance, her voice, her very name would be changed. Nick was being paid to create a fantasy. But what did he think about the reality? What did he think about her?

Chapter Four

Nick sucked in a deep breath, inhaling her alluring scent. This was the very situation he was hoping to avoid. And the very situation he dreamed about. Standing so close, pinned to the wall by nothing more than the warmth of her body and an invisible hold she seemed to have over him. He out-classed her in both weight and strength, yet he couldn't move away for the life of him.

"So, what now?" she asked quietly, breaking into his thoughts.

He knew he should stop. She was leaving the next move up to him. If he was smart, he would politely extract himself and get back to work but business was the furthest thing from his mind. For the first time in a long time, desire ruled his actions.

He slid his hands around her back. She inched closer, brushing against him. Passionate and beautiful, an intoxicating combination. One he thought he was immune to. Why couldn't he walk away?

He gazed into her clear blue eyes. Desire, hope, and a growing senses of curiosity seemed to be reflected in them. There was no pretense to Alexis. She didn't hide what she wanted. He wasn't used to that kind of openness from a woman and he felt defenseless against it.

Her warm breath caressed his cheek. Their lips met in a tender, yet surprisingly heated kiss. His pulse jumped. She tasted as sweet as she looked. The inclination to surrender himself in the moment and forget the consequences was almost more than he could fight. Almost.

When he was about to surrender, a spark of déjà vu restored his failing reason. Never again would he let hormones rule his actions in a relationship. Especially with Alexis. There was too much at stake for both of them to complicate their arrangement with sex. At the same time, he didn't want to alienate her and end up fighting her every step of the way. He could use their attraction to his advantage, but only if he remained in complete control. Rather than extract himself from the situation, it was time to take command.

Nick inched Alexis closer until he enfolded her in a steely embrace. She felt safe and sheltered, and those were two things she hadn't felt in a long time. She could get used to this.

His kiss unleashed a yearning she had long kept dormant. A relationship had been last on her list of priorities because of her hectic life. Yet with his offer, he had turned both her professional and her personal world upside down. He deserved to be at least as off balance as he had made her. And right now, she was down right shaky in the knees.

She gazed at Nick. To her disappointment, he seemed in complete control of his emotions. She inhaled deeply, trying to restore her equilibrium. It was obvious he knew how to get to her. But how could she get to someone who held an ironfisted rein over his emotions? He could not be as unaffected as he appeared, could he?

"Have you gotten it out of your system now, Princess?" His voice came out in a husky whisper against her ear and sent a shiver along her spine. He wasn't completely immune, he just hid his emotions better than she.

"For the time being."

"Are you telling me it isn't over?" he asked.

"You know it's not."

"I stand warned." His tone was one of amusement rather than annoyance.

"You don't believe me?" she asked.

"I believe that you believe it. But you will soon realize the wisdom of maintaining a professional relationship."

"Well, that would be wise . . . if I worked for you." Alexis walked into the living room and curled up in the corner of the leather sofa. She needed to come up with a better game plan when dealing with him. "But I am employed and paid by Mr. Costas. So, to answer your earlier question, there is no other man in my life. And *you* made this personal rather than professional when you asked."

Nick shook his head. He didn't argue the point but neither did he admit it. Why was he so guarded? He wanted her, she had felt it in his kiss. What could be simpler than two people who were mutually attracted, exploring the possibilities?

He took his car keys from his pocket, readying himself for a quick exit. "Do you need anything before I leave?"

"Do you live around here?" she asked.

He arched his eyebrow skeptically. "Why?"

She let out a soft laugh. "Oh, don't worry. I'm not going to start stalking you. I just wanted to know where the nearest food store is located."

"There are probably a hundred take-out places within a three block radius."

"I'm sure there are." That didn't mean she was going to start living the life of a spoiled princess one moment before she had to. Between the taxes that were taken from her first check and the up-front costs she had paid the nursing facility for her grandmother, she wasn't left with money to burn this month. "I happen to like to cook."

"I don't think there are any grocery stores in this immediate area. I could run you downtown."

"Never mind. The delivery van will be here with my stuff soon. I'll grab a burger later. Tomorrow, I can figure out what's where."

"If you're sure."

She didn't want him to leave her alone in the sterile apartment, but neither would she beg him to stay. Her feelings for Nick were too new and too confusing. In light of his determination to keep his emotions uninvolved, she would be smart to try to do the same. "I'm sure."

* * *

Nick strode down Fifth Avenue, maneuvering his way through the normal weekday crowds of yuppies, students, and tourists. The subways rumbled beneath his feet and car horns blared impatiently. Only when he approached the public parking garage did he break stride and walk at a normal pace. What had he been thinking?

He could handle her. He could remain in control. He'd had about as much restraint as a kid in a candy store on allowance day. He reminded himself that she was a princess and a key player in his advertising campaign. She might be honest and unspoiled now, but he knew it wouldn't last. When she got a taste of wealth, when she discovered the power of her beauty, she would want more. He'd seen it before.

He and Costas were about to turn her into everything he disliked in a woman. A sophisticated, cool beauty who could get any man she set her sights on. Once her transformation was complete, they would *all* cash in on her looks. Wasn't that the point of the entire campaign? To convince the customer that Royal Blue and the House of Yanis could make any woman a sensual, desirable princess lusted after by kings and commoners alike? *Sex sells!* It was the first commandment of advertising.

He had used the device effectively in the past without a second thought.

He handed the parking attendant his ticket stub and impatiently waited for his car. Why the sudden bout of conscience? Alexis knew what she was getting herself into. He had been honest with her from the beginning. She had taken the money. He wasn't going to lose his career or his heart to another woman who placed a dollar amount on her worth. Been there, done that. But somewhere in the far recesses of his cynical mind, a small part of him couldn't help but think there was more to Alexis' decision than greed or self indulgence.

Alexis glanced around the living room. With her pictures and knickknacks placed strategically in the apartment, the place didn't seem as impersonal as it had earlier. Of course, it had felt a whole lot warmer when Nick had been there. Now there was a man who could turn heads. Forget those scrawny model types whose underwear ads graced the pages of fashion magazines. Nick's tall, muscular build radiated strength and his aloof manner made him an irresistible challenge.

Maybe he was right. The next few months were going to be confusing enough. Did she really want to complicate her life with a one-sided relationship?

She wasn't the type to indulge in a purely physical affair and walk away unscathed. For now, she had enough to do with learning what was to be expected of her. She had no experience in either the fashion world or advertising. Her free time would be better spent probing Nick's mind rather than flirting with him. Not as fun, perhaps, but safer for her peace of mind.

Despite her new resolve, she couldn't seem to get her mind off Nick for the rest of the afternoon. She had never been on her own before and the loneliness left her with too much time to think. About Nick. About her grandmother. And about Nick again. It wasn't as if she had never dated a man before. So why couldn't she banish the memory of his kiss? Why did her heart flutter at the thought of him?

Life just wasn't fair, she decided, as she unpacked her clothes. She had finally found a man who could light her fire and he wanted to douse out the flame. She chuckled at the irony. Her life had been full enough without a man until now. All she had to do was stop thinking about him.

By the time Marissa arrived after her work shift, Alexis was in dire need of a distraction.

"Wow," Marissa marveled as she toured the apartment. "You've even got closet space which beats the heck out of most Manhattan apartments. You really stepped into it."

Her friend seemed to forget that this was a temporary reversal of fortune. Once the campaign was over and done with, the Princess of Montavia would go back to being a working girl from Brighton Beach. "The leather furniture is as soft as butter."

Marissa grinned as she flopped into the overstuffed couch. "It's great for snuggling on."

"Personal experience or did you read that in the current issue of *Cosmo*?"

"You mean you haven't tried it out yet?"

Alexis nearly choked. "What?"

"The way Mr. Madison Avenue was eyeing you, I figured he would have showed you his sofa technique already."

"Very funny." She wasn't about to admit that his technique against the wall was more than enough excitement for one day. Especially when she had already decided that an affair with Nick was a fool-hearted dream. "There is nothing between me and Mr. Lanborne."

"I'm not blind, Lexie. You've got it bad for him and you know it."

"He's not looking to become involved with me."

"Who said anything about getting involved? I was talking about a steamy, get-it-out-of-your-system affair."

"Dating tips for the new millennium?" Alexis laughed. "Call me old fashioned, but I still want a little romance with my relationship."

Marissa crinkled her nose. "If you're looking for a kind, sensitive, caring man to sweep you off your feet, then I have to warn you, those guys only exist in movies. All the rest are Neanderthals."

Alexis chuckled at her friend's apt assessment of the male gene pool. "Worry about your own love life and I'll worry about mine."

She raked back a handful of frosted hair from her face and grinned. "You gotta have one before I could worry about it."

Before Alexis could find a suitable comeback, the doorbell rang. She looked toward her smirking friend and shrugged. The only other person who knew where she lived was Nick. Her stomach somersaulted. She smoothed her hair and straightened her clothes.

"Oh, right. There's nothing between you . . ." Marissa muttered as Alexis opened the door.

Disappointment caused the air to rush from her lungs. It wasn't Nick on the other side of the door, but instead a delivery boy holding a large paper bag. "Your dinner, Miss Marks."

How did this young kid know her name? "I didn't order anything," she mumbled.

"Well, somebody did and paid for it too."

She shot a glance toward Marissa.

"Not me," she said, snapping her gum. "Must be some other disinterested person who knows your address and would think to send you dinner. Gee, who might that be?"

Without acknowledging the comment, Alexis took the bag and tipped the young man. While unloading the Styrofoam containers onto the kitchen table, the rich aromas caused her mouth to water. At the bottom of the bag was the receipt listing the contents. Dishes like borscht and goulash, as well as several dishes she'd never heard of. A note scribbled across the back said, "Consider this the beginning of your education, Princess."

Only Nick would take a nice gesture and turn it into business. He knew she had no food and went out of his way to find a place that made Eastern European fare. To be sure she didn't read anything into his lapse of kindness, he attached his note to remind her she was just another business deduction.

Chapter Five

On Monday, Nick's morning had been tied up with several meetings, but he made his way to the Costas showroom by late afternoon. He sat in a quiet, back corner. His seat allowed him to watch the action without being seen himself. Alexis was twisting herself into a slinky red number, and by the looks of things, she wasn't going to make it. One of the staff, a perky blond design student, tried to fasten the zipper from behind.

"Suck in," Yanis ordered in an exasperated voice.

"I could empty all the air from my lungs and this glorified slip still wouldn't fit. No freaking way. Forget about it! I'm not a size zero. It needs to be resized."

Nick grinned. She was not one of those anorexic fashion models. She was a delicate combination of rounded curves, a narrow waist and mile long legs.

"And something else . . ." she said.

Yanis let out a tirade in Greek, smiling all the while. Despite the work tension, there seemed to be a kind of sibling bond of affection between Yanis and Alexis.

"Yo, Yanis. I'm talkin' to you."

"If the word *yo*, comes out of your pretty little mouth one more time, I'll have you gagged. And lose that word *freaking* from your vocabulary. What kind of princess goes around talking like that?"

She tossed her hands in the air and pirouetted to show off the dress. "What kind of princess goes around dressed like she works for an escort service?"

"Maybe if you got rid of the bubble gum, you wouldn't look like an escort."

"Maybe if you rethought the dress, I wouldn't either. The neckline is too low and the hemline is to high."

"Are you going to tell me how to do my job now, Lexie?"

"All right, then explain to me why I need a

red mini-dress when the product is called Royal Blue." She slipped out of the garment and handed it back to Costas. As she stood there, in just her lacy slip, Nick had to fight the urge to cross the showroom floor and cover her body. First he had to get his own body under control.

"Help me out here, Nick," Costas called out.

Alexis let out a small gasp and grabbed for the silk robe draped over a chair. Apparently she hadn't noticed his arrival. Why was she suddenly shy in front of him when she'd had no problem standing around in her lingerie in front of Costas?

"I'd like to, but I have to agree with her. Something a bit more understated would give the aristocratic look we discussed. And her comment about the color makes sense. You want the customer to tie her image to the product."

Arms folded across her chest, she sent a grateful nod in his direction. "Listen to the man, he's an advertising genius."

Costas laughed. "Funny, I got the impression you thought he was nuts for thinking we could turn you into a princess. *Now* he's a genius?"

Alexis shot a silencing glare at the designer. Nick could only guess what else she might have told her new buddy. His behavior the last time they were together had been erratic at best. He hadn't acted like a man who wanted to keep a professional relationship. And a weekend of distance hadn't changed his perspective. As she stood before him, clutching her robe and her skin flushed with a healthy glow, he found himself reacting to her in a way that bothered him.

Costas cleared his throat. If he noticed the chemistry at work, he chose not to mention the fact. "And besides, she can't have an entire wardrobe of blue."

Her expression changed to one of confusion, tinged with sorrow. "Who said anything about an entire wardrobe? I thought I just needed clothes for the magazine layout and public appearances."

Any other woman would be ecstatic at the prospect of an entire new wardrobe. His ex would have killed for the chance at a complete designer collection. But Alexis wasn't like his ex or like any other woman for that matter.

"There will be a lot of public appearances in the beginning," Nick said.

She looked even less pleased. "How many is *a lot*?"

Nick shook his head. He didn't *get* her. If she wasn't in this for material reasons, and she wasn't searching for instant fame, why had she signed on? Despite a dossier of information collected on her, he realized that he knew nothing about Alexis. But he wanted to. She intrigued him. It had been a long time since something other than business had sparked his interest.

"Why don't we all discuss this over dinner?" Nick suggested.

"I have plans." Costas winked at Alexis. "You fight it out . . . I mean, work it out with him. I'll have the dress resized."

"Yanis . . ." she groaned.

"Red is your color, darling, despite the name of the product. It's the color of aggression. In that dress, you will be more willing to go after what you want."

"In that dress, I'll have what I *don't* want coming after me," she muttered as she stomped away.

He watched her retreat to the changing room. The soft sway of her hips coupled with the long stride of her shapely legs held his attention until the door closed behind her. Then he glanced at his amused client.

"What?" he asked.

Costas shrugged. "Nothing. Enjoy your dinner."

"It's just business."

"Right. And Alexis Markova is just like any fashion model you've used in a photo shoot."

They both knew that was a lie as well. Alexis wasn't like anyone he'd ever dealt with in the business. She needed special handling and sensitivity, which was more Costas' forte than Nick's. Only his client was leaving the personal problems to him and, equipped or not, Nick had to deal with them. So how could he convince her that she needed to make herself over completely, when he found her so irresistible the way she was?

Alexis changed back into her denim shorts and tee-shirt. Slipping her feet into a pair of flip-flops, she left the dressing room. Her nerves were stretched to the limit. If not for her visit yesterday to her grandmother, to remind her why she was doing this, she might have chucked it all. Nana seemed content in her new home. She was around people her own age, and Riverdale's policy of keeping the residents as active as possible meant she wasn't wasting her days away. Still, Alexis felt guilty that she had placed her grandmother in a home at all and even more guilty about exploiting the family name to pay for it. Her only consolation was that Nana would never know.

When she walked back into the showroom the two men were off in a corner, apparently discussing her, since they both stopped the second they saw her. Nick, in his standard pin-striped suit with white shirt, and Yanis, dressed in black pleated pants and a melon colored shirt, couldn't look more different. Their personalities were polar opposites as well. Yanis was warm and funny. Nick was serious and aloof. Their only common bond was a desire to turn her into something she didn't want to be. Well, she had signed the contract so she had to stop fighting the process.

She slipped the strap of her handbag over her head and waited by the door for Nick. He joined her a moment later and followed her up the one flight of stairs to the apartment.

"If you don't mind, I'd rather not go out. I'm expecting a call." She dropped her purse on a leather recliner. "I could cook dinner for us."

Nick hovered in the foyer. "Perhaps you'd rather be alone when you get the call. You are on your own time now."

Actually, she wasn't sure she wanted the call at all. The nursing home physicians had run a battery of tests on her grandmother, and she was waiting to hear back from them on Nana's prognosis. She prayed for the best and feared the worst. However, Nick didn't know that. His assumption that she needed privacy for her call, and his tension-filled stance made him appear jealous. Did he think she had a lover? And why would he care who she received calls from when he wasn't interested in her himself?

"If I wanted to be alone, I wouldn't have offered you dinner. After working in a bar, I know how to tell a man to get lost when I want to."

"All right. I'll stay."

"Good. I owe you for the food you sent the other night. I didn't get a chance to thank you." She stepped into the kitchen while Nick took a seat at the oak breakfast bar.

"I hope you enjoyed it," he said.

"I did. And so did my grandmother." She only wished that she understood what Nana had been saying at certain times during the visit. Her brief rambling in a language alien to Alexis had left her worried about her grandmother's mental condition.

"I'm sure it wasn't nearly as good as she remembered from her childhood."

"She seemed to think it was. Anyway, you didn't come here to discuss my grandmother." She pulled a pot from a cabinet and filled it with water. "I realize now that I should have asked a lot more questions before I decided to let you and Yanis take over my life."

He loosened the tie knotted at his throat. "Ask away, Princess."

"Just a second." Opening the refrigerator, she took jars containing sun-dried tomatoes, capers, and two fresh Portobello mushrooms out and placed them on the counter. "Okay. First of all, what kind of public appearances are you talking about? The contract wasn't specific."

"Fashion events and charity balls mostly. Most times you'll attend as Costas' date."

"You guys even supply me with the dates?" She sighed. Did she own any part of her life? "Lucky me. I suppose I could do worse. After all, he's handsome, charming, and sensitive."

Nick's eyes narrowed. "He's involved with someone."

"No kidding?" Her voice pitched in mock surprise.

"You knew."

"He told me. So, why go out with me?"

"To get you, and his new product, exposure. In fact, people will probably believe that you are one of his wealthy benefactors."

She grinned at the irony. "When in reality, it's the other way around."

He rolled his broad shoulders in a shrug. "Perception is everything."

"In your world."

"It is now your world too, Alexis. The sooner you accept it, the easier it will be."

She lowered her head sadly, because she knew he was right. The success of the campaign depended a lot on Nick's ingenuity, but also on how Princess Alexis Markova was presented to the media. Still, for her own self-respect, she had to hold onto a part of Lexie Marks. And that was the part she wanted to share with him. Nick had taken a big risk with her professionally. Why wouldn't he take a little risk with her personally?

Nick watched Alexis while she cooked. She was obviously no stranger to the kitchen. He had trouble reconciling this domestic image of her with that of a pampered princess he wanted to create. Alexis didn't go out of her way to make an impression, and that alone impressed him.

Her lack of pretense wasn't the only thing about her that he admired. What her athletic shape did for a pair of shorts defied description!

What really scared him, however, was how much he enjoyed the intimacy of the situation. He couldn't remember the last time a woman had cooked for him. The simple act of watching her work gave him a sense of longing he hadn't known in a long time. They didn't speak, but it was a comfortable silence. So comfortable, in fact, that it made him uncomfortable. This was no time to lapse into an Ozzie and Harriet fantasy.

When the food was ready, Alexis stepped around the granite counter and into the dining room to set the table. She stretched up high to reach the glasses on the top shelf of a china hutch. As he came up behind her to give her a hand, he was surrounded by her familiar scent that had haunted him for the past week. His fascination with her was completely out of character. In the past, the only thing to get him excited was a new client signing on the proverbial dotted line. How had this woman gotten under his skin with so little effort on her part?

At some point, she had gone from being an abstract commodity to a living, breathing, female. And he was on the verge of breaking his ironclad rule about mixing business with pleasure.

Chapter Six

Alexis gazed into Nick's green eyes, looking for some sign this was a joke, waiting for a punch line. She shifted her weight between her feet. What was he doing? Just when she decided to give him up as a lost cause, he pulled a u-turn without signaling first. Men like Nick were the reason most women considered joining a convent at some point in their lives.

"Would you rather I didn't?" His husky words vibrated slowly against her ear.

"Didn't what?"

"Kiss you."

She shrugged nonchalantly but her heart was racing with excitement. Trying for the cool and sophisticated demeanor he seemed to prefer when she felt like going wild was no easy task. "I don't know, Nick. Dessert before dinner might spoil my appetite."

He shook his head in exasperation. "Is that a yes or a no?"

She swallowed hard. Of course she wanted him to kiss her. Nick was the one who seemed undecided. She wasn't sure if she was flattered or insulted by his obvious internal struggle concerning her. "Interpret it how you want."

"I think . . ." He paused in his usual fashion to weigh his options.

"That's your problem. You think too much." She placed her hands on his shoulders and gave him a gentle push into the chair behind him. "Dinner's getting cold."

Before she could turn away, he grabbed the waistband of her shorts and hauled her into his lap. "I like my spaghetti cold."

The shrill ring of the phone startled them both. Nick's deep grunt echoed her own. After flying in the clouds, her reentry to earth was abrupt and frustrating.

His expression was hard to read. Disappointment, certainly, but she thought she saw a trace of relief in his schooled features as well.

"Are you going to get that?" he asked.

"The machine . . ."

"Weren't you waiting for a call?"

His words doused her faster than a bucket of ice water. She slid from his lap and sprinted into the living room before the answering machine could pick up.

Nick shuddered and slouched down in the chair. Thank goodness her call arrived when it had! He had come too close to surrendering his body and soul, and he couldn't afford that luxury. Sex was a physical need, not an emotional one. With Alexis the line had blurred. She had managed to breach his defenses a second time. He couldn't allow a third.

He glanced into the living room. Alexis was cradling the phone against her cheek while twisting her hands together nervously.

"May I speak with him?" she asked the caller. As she paused to listen, he watched her grow more tense. "How can you tell me not to worry when her condition is too complicated to discuss over the phone . . ."

She paced back and forth across the Persian carpet. Her moisture filled eyes shimmered under the track lighting. "Okay, then I want to come in now . . . not tomorrow . . . what time does he finish rounds? . . . I'll be there." She dropped the phone back onto the base.

"I have to go." Without meeting his gaze,

she grabbed her purse from the chair. "The food is ready. Feel free to eat something before you leave . . ."

"I'll give you a ride."

She shook her head to decline the offer. Normally he wouldn't make a second offer but she was visibly shaken and in no condition to be going out on her own. He wasn't trying to spend more time with her, nor was he looking to get involved in her personal life. He had to look out for his investment. That's what he told himself, anyway.

"I'm driving you."

"It's not necessary."

He slid his arm across her back and led her toward the door. "Deal with it, Princess, people are going to be doing things for you now. Just accept the offer graciously and say thank you."

"More educational pointers?" she muttered under her breath. "And stop calling me Princess."

He tipped his head. "Your wish is my command."

Through her anxiety and tension, she still managed a small smile. "Can we go please?"

"Your chariot awaits."

"Stop breaking my chops, Nick, before I throw a royal fit."

If he was honest, he would admit that he wasn't teasing her, he was reminding himself of his place. He respected her down-to-earth ways and her determination to distance herself from the public persona they were trying to create. Nothing was real for her yet. But she would change once Princess Alexis was officially introduced to society. There was no way that kind of money and attention would leave her unaffected. If he prepared himself for that eventuality from the beginning, he wouldn't be disappointed by her later.

Alexis waited outside the doctor's office with Nick at her side. She had told him she didn't need a ride to the nursing home. She had told him he didn't need to walk her inside. She had even told him it wasn't necessary to wait with her. Thankfully, the man hadn't listened to her. Despite the fact that he hadn't said a word since they walked in the front door, his presence comforted her.

Nick was an enigma. For a man who claimed he wanted to keep a cool distance, he had certainly delivered one hot kiss. Her body still tingled from the memory. She wondered what his story was. Costas had offered to share some gossip regarding Nick, but she'd refused. If there was dirt to share, then someone had hurt him, but it wasn't her business unless Nick chose to tell her.

Still, she was curious about him. He insisted on staying with her, yet he seemed uncomfortable in the nursing home surroundings. Riverdale was nicer than most of them, so it couldn't be the warm and friendly environment that bothered him. Why was he here? Nick wasn't big on sensitivity. Nor was he a great communicator. Her grandmother had always told her not to ask questions if she didn't really want the answer. He was here, and it was enough.

A nurse stepped into the waiting room. "Miss Marks. Doctor Poufour will see you now."

Alexis' heart hammered in her chest. Her grandmother was all the family she had left in the world. She had watched Nana's condition deteriorate over the past six months so she feared the news was not going to be good.

"I'll wait here for you," Nick said.

She sent him a grateful smile then followed the nurse down a small corridor and into an office. The room was bright like the reception area, with soothing landscapes adorning the walls. Diplomas for the several physicians who shared the office were framed and hung behind a large mahogany desk. She stood on the opposite side of the desk from the gray haired man and waited for him to look up from the file he was reading. His white coat and stethoscope gave him stature despite his diminutive size.

"Have a seat," he said.

"Thank you." She slid into the leather chair with a swoosh.

"It wasn't necessary to rush down here tonight, Miss Marks."

"Alexis," she corrected. "And it was necessary for me."

His serious demeanor didn't help to put her at ease. "Then let me get to the point. Nadianna Marks shouldn't be in this facility."

"What do you mean?" A giant knot formed in the pit of her stomach. His bedside manner could use some work. She didn't want to be patronized but he could have eased into his announcement. "Her condition is that far advanced?"

His bushy brow arched in question. "What condition? Your grandmother is in relatively good health considering her age."

Alexis shook her head. "Forgive me doctor, but I've been living with her. This past couple of months she's become disoriented, her memory is slipping and she's lethargic. I don't call that relatively good health."

"She sufferers from several age related ailments, like elevated blood pressure and arthritis. And her heart is slowing down a bit."

"It has to be more than that. Her home health aid thought she was exhibiting early signs of Alzheimer's."

"Her home health aid should have left the diagnosis to a qualified doctor instead of worrying you needlessly."

Alexis had left the diagnoses to the supposedly qualified primary care physician and emergency room doctors and Nana kept getting worse. Was she now supposed to believe nothing was wrong? "I've seen the signs myself."

Dr. Poufour glanced at the chart again. "It is my belief that her symptoms are not caused by a decline in health, but by a conflict in her medications. While relieving her physical ailments, the medications taken together have caused other problems."

For several seconds she stared in numbed shock, trying to comprehend his meaning. When the words sunk in, her blood boiled with anger. "Why wasn't that picked up sooner? I've had her back and forth to doctors almost weekly in the past two months, and they were all fully aware of the medications that she was taking. They would just increase the dosage and tell me that her symptoms were age related."

He shuffled the papers, looking distinctly uncomfortable. "I'm really not familiar with the case."

Alexis knew that an unspoken code among doctors would forbid the physician from making any statement that might be misconstrued as malpractice on a colleague's part. "So, what is the next step?"

"If I'm correct about her condition, my suggestion is that she be moved to our senior housing facility. There is a nurse on staff to monitor her new medications. But she would have her own living quarters, with her personal belongings around her. She could avail herself to the game room, spa, and cafeteria on the premises as well as take day trips all over the city and all at considerably less than the nursing home rate. In fact, her social security and pension would most likely cover the bulk of the expense."

Alexis' head was spinning. Mixed emotions washed over her in waves. She had been so prepared for the worst that her mind and body couldn't react to the good news. Especially when her grandmother's condition should have been detected and prevented months ago. Part of her wanted to sing with relief and another part wanted to throttle the doctors who had made such a dangerous mistake.

"You don't need to make any decisions right now. I want to keep her here at least a few more days to see how she responds to the new meds. Even once we change her medications, it will take a good month before the old drugs are completely out of her system. In the meantime you can meet with the administrative department and decide what you want to do."

"Could I take her home?" Alexis asked.

"That's your decision. In familiar surroundings she would thrive just as well."

What was she thinking? There were no familiar surroundings anymore. She had given up her Brooklyn apartment, and she wouldn't be willing to meet her old landlord's "personal" terms for returning. Her current apartment, which only had one bedroom, didn't even belong to her in the legal sense of the word, although she was sure Costas wouldn't care if she brought her grandmother to stay with her there. Nor did it have the amenities the doctor had listed. Although she wanted Nana with her, her new apartment wouldn't benefit her grandmother the way the senior center could.

Then there was the matter of Nick. Whether or not her grandmother needed the services of Riverdale, he had given Alexis the opportunity and the means to pay for that security. And she had signed a contract in return. Her circumstances might have changed, but that didn't give her the right to walk away from the business deal now. She'd given her word. She was committed to follow through. And if she was honest, she wasn't ready to walk away from the man either.

Chapter Seven

One hour later, Nick brought Alexis back to the apartment. She hadn't spoken on the ride back and he hadn't asked questions. If she wanted to talk he figured she would have said something. He wasn't going to pry into her business. She deserved her privacy, or so he told himself.

His conscience mocked him. To ask would be to get involved in her life. He wasn't looking for a long-term relationship with shared confidences that were supposed to bring couples closer together, but actually only gave them ammunition to use against each other. His father thought he'd had something deep and special with his mother, and the old man busted his back to give her everything she wanted. In the end, it wasn't enough. She left his father, and Nick. But not before her torrid affair with a local handyman created a scandal in their upper-class suburban town.

Since then, he hadn't met a woman who wasn't out for herself. Of course a shrink would probably say he gravitated toward that kind of woman to prove his point that all women were selfish.

Alexis was different, but no less dangerous to his peace of mind. She made him want to disregard his hard-learned lessons. The fact remained that her life was in the midst of a major upheaval and she had yet to experience the world that was about to open up for her. He made a good living, but Nick didn't kid himself. His salary wasn't near the stratosphere of the men who would soon be paying court to the princess.

"I guess I should be going," he said.

Alexis shook her head as if she hadn't heard. Her blue-eyed stare gave her a vulnerability that melted the block of ice he called his heart. How could he walk out now, when she looked so lost? How could he stay and not lose himself?

"It will only take a sec to reheat the food," she barely muttered.

"You're probably exhausted."

"Shell-shocked is a better word." She trans-
ferred the food from a pot to a large serving
bowl. "But still hungry. I promised you dinner.
So have a seat in the dining room."

While compassion wasn't his strongest suit,
he wasn't completely insensitive. If her distracted demeanor was anything to judge by,
she had been through something distressing
and she wanted company. After dinner he
could make a tactical retreat.

During the meal, Alexis drank more wine
than she was obviously used to. Along with
the rosy glow in her cheeks, there was a
change in her mood as well. She babbled on
about inconsequential matters, with both
humor and wit. She was entertaining and
engaging. Everything a perfect hostess should
be. Nick didn't buy her turnabout. She was
overcompensating, working too hard at
appearing happy to actually be happy. The
bouncing two-step she danced while cleaning
the dishes and the silly tunes she hummed
seemed to be nothing more than a cover.
Whenever her gaze turned toward a picture of
her family, she recoiled in pain.

She was a woman in need of a good cry. He
was a man who didn't like to deal with emotions. So instead of encouraging her to open

up, he pretended to be fooled by her little charade.

When she finished in the kitchen, she waltzed into the living room to join him. She spun around once and stood directly in front of him. "Dance with me, Nick."

"I think you need to sit down for a while."

She draped her arms around his neck. "No. Yanis said I have to learn ballroom dancing."

"There will be time for that later." He slipped from her gentle hold and took a step back. "Right now, you should rest."

"I'd much rather tango. And it takes two." She grinned and he was almost tempted to take her up on her flirtatious offer. If it hadn't been the wine talking, he might have.

He cupped his hand along the side of her face. His thumb stroked her soft cheek. "I know you've had some bad news regarding your grandmother, but this isn't the way to deal with it."

She shook her head. "I didn't have bad news. I had very good news."

"You did?"

"Yes, my grandmother is in very good health. So good that they don't feel she needs the services of the Riverdale Center."

Her voice didn't ring with the joy that news should have brought. He didn't understand,

and surprisingly he wanted to. Her life couldn't have been going any better. She and her grandmother were both healthy. She was financially sound and living virtually expense free for the next two years.

So, what was wrong? He knew he shouldn't ask. Once he became involved in her life, there was no turning back. "What's the problem?"

Tears shimmered in her eyes. She hugged her arms around her waist in a gesture that seemed to offer no comfort.

"The problem is, the doctors should have discovered the cause of her symptoms *before* she had to be admitted to Riverdale. Before I gave up our rent controlled apartment." She shuddered and turned away as if she could conceal her sorrow, but it rang too clearly in her voice. "Before I had to figure out a way to tell her that I signed away her heritage to pay for it."

For sheer discomfort, a kick to the groin would have ached less. Of all the theories he had come up with regarding Alexis' motives for signing on, that one had never crossed his mind. She had given up everything—her job, her home, her very freedom—to ensure her grandmother's security. In her position, his offer had amounted to little more than blackmail. He wasn't feeling too good about his professional coup right now.

What was he supposed to do? Her contract was not with him, but with Yanis Costas. "I suppose I could talk to Costas about a different ad campaign . . ."

"No!" She whirled around, stumbled, and grabbed his shoulders.

He splayed his hands over her hips, holding onto her even after she caught her balance. The smell of her, a combination of lemon soap and floral perfume, kicked his hormones up a notch. "This obviously isn't what you want to be doing."

"I gave my word."

"Under duress," he added.

"You weren't holding a gun to my head. In fact, you were very honest about what I was getting myself into before I signed the contract."

He wished she had been as forthcoming about her reasons for accepting in the first place. Not that they would have made a bit of difference to him at the time. He would have done whatever it took to land the account, even exploiting her situation.

The ache in his gut became acute. When had he developed a conscience? Not only a conscience, but feelings for Alexis as well. This was not part of his meticulous plan. He was supposed to find her, sign her, and then walk away with his payment in hand. He certainly had no intention of becoming involved in her private life.

"Besides, you don't have another princess waiting in the wings. And I'd feel even worse if I let Yanis down. I made a commitment and I plan to do my part to the end." Her lips pursed in a determined pout.

Although he would understand if she took him up on his offer, his own reputation was at stake if she bolted. Lucky for him, that wasn't her style. He knew by the way he had handled her last employer that Alexis honored her commitments.

His admiration for her continued to grow. As did his desire. It was time for a quick exit before he did something stupid like pulling her into his arms and kissing her. Bad enough, he was using her professionally for personal gain. He wasn't going to exploit her attraction to him as well. She deserved so much more emotionally than he would ever be able to give her.

Alexis sat in the chaise lounge and stared out the bedroom window at the street below. Flashing neon lights beckoned her but she wasn't in a partying mood. Since Nick's departure two days earlier, she hadn't seen or heard from him. Between fittings, salon visits, and preliminary photo sessions, she had been kept very busy, but he was still noticeably absent. She had probably scared him off. Why had she unburdened her problems on him? She had only served to make him uncomfortable.

Nick had been very honest with her from the beginning, both about the job and about any kind of relationship between them. That didn't stop her from wanting him. Or from deluding herself into believing that given the chance, she could relieve him of some of the excess baggage he seemed to be hauling around with him. However, the odds weren't in her favor when he deliberately avoided her.

She had to stop thinking about him all the time. Even Marissa's presence and her irreverent chatter couldn't derail Alexis' one-track train of thought. She glanced at her friend, sitting at the vanity to apply her makeup.

"Are you going to get dressed so we can go out, or are you going to sit there mooning over him all night?" Marissa finally asked.

Alexis feigned indifference. "Who?"

"You know who. Your boss."

"Costas?"

Marissa snapped her gum in annoyance. "The other one."

"There's nothing between us," Alexis said with a wave of her hand.

"Lexie, this is me you're trying to lie to. The man makes you excited just thinking about him."

Heat rushed to her cheeks. "What kind of talk is that?"

Marissa arched her eyebrow in question. "Have you become too good for mere mortal yearnings, Your Highness?"

Alexis rose from the lounger and paced the hardwood floor. The princess cracks were wearing thin on all fronts. She was still the same person she was a month ago. "That's not funny, even as a joke."

"Yeah, I know. So, just admit that you're hot and bothered. I'm not buying this cool and detached bit you're trying to sell."

"I like him a lot, but the closer I try to get, the more he backs away."

"You need to pin him down."

"How?"

Marissa grinned like a Cheshire cat. "Handcuffs work well."

Alexis shook her head. "I should have known better than to try to have a serious conversation with you."

"Jeepers, Lexie, you really do have it bad for him." Marissa put a comforting arm around her shoulder. "I wish I could help, but my track record with men isn't exactly a good one. I'd say something trite, like 'just be your-self,' but hey, they're spending a fortune to turn you into something else."

Marissa's comment, although not meant to be cruel, cut deeply. Alexis couldn't get used to the changes. She ran her fingers through her shorter hair. She had stopped looking in mirrors since returning from the Fifth Avenue salon because she couldn't get used to her reflection. A line of feathery bangs minimized her long forehead. The angles of the cut framed her face and earth tone colors made her eyes seem larger and more expressive. She'd never realized what makeup could accomplish in the hands of a master.

Marissa's suggestion that she try out the new look with some bar-hopping had seemed like a good idea an hour ago, but when it came down to it, Alexis wasn't up for a night on the town. She had left that lifestyle to take care of her grandmother, and in truth, she hadn't missed it.

"Marissa . . ."

"Let me guess," her friend began. "You'd rather break out a package of Oreos and a box of tissues, and watch *Roman Holiday.*"

"If you wouldn't mind."

"It will just upset you. The princess doesn't get her man in the end of the movie, either."

"Maybe not. But at least she had one magical night with him." Alexis would settle for that.

Nick glanced through a small stack of photographs. He barely recognized the woman in the pictures as Alexis. Her dark hair had been styled in a collar length blunt cut with a wisp of bangs that drew attention to her wide round eyes. The strapless gown in royal blue silk draped her feminine curves in a manner that caused his blood pressure to rise.

She was photogenic, he had no worries there. Her ability to convey a wide range of emotions for the camera made his job that much easier. Her natural grace and beauty took care of the rest. Costas was creating a masterpiece, a work of art that would be admired by many. If only he could shake the feeling that what they were doing was wrong. Despite Alexis' insistence to honor her contract, he believed she had been unduly influenced in her decision.

Dolores knocked on his open office door before entering. "Is there anything else you need before I leave, Mr. Lanborne?"

He straightened the pictures back into a neat pile. "You can file these."

She took the stack from him. "Do you mind if I have a look?"

"No."

Nick watched her expression. He knew from personal experience how a man would react to Alexis, but he was interested in a woman's opinion, since that was the target market he was aiming for. And his no-nonsense office manager would be bluntly honest.

"She is lovely, isn't she? And Yanis Costas' designs certainly give her an elegant air," Dolores said.

"But does she capture your attention?"

"How could she not? She is stunning, without making a woman feel insecure the way many super skinny supermodels do. And she's so . . ."

"Regal? Royal?"

She tapped a finger against the edge of the picture. "Well, yes, very elegant. But something more."

"What?"

"I'm not sure I can put my finger on it."

"Cool and aloof?"

"Not at all. She seems vulnerable and lonely, which is perfect for that untouchable image you are going for, but sad for a twenty-five-year-old woman who has the world at her feet."

"She won't be lonely for long once the campaign is underway," he grumbled with an uncharacteristic blast of jealousy.

"Attention is not a cure for loneliness. I would have thought you knew that by now."

Nick didn't miss the reproach in the older woman's voice. Dolores was aware of certain details in his life that he wished were private. In a small office it was hard to have total privacy. Especially when his mother poured her heart out to his personal assistant when he didn't have time to deal with her.

He found it difficult to believe his mother had acted out of loneliness when she had walked out on her husband and son. She had had everything a woman could want—a house, a family, and a community of friends—but still, she had left. And for what? Life in a rented apartment with a blue collar laborer. At least Nick's ex-fiancé had jilted him for a richer man. Greed he understood.

Alexis, however, was entitled to live the good life. She had sacrificed her own happiness to put her family first. It was her turn and she deserved all the attention she had coming.

Tension blanketed his body like a shroud. He hated the idea of her cavorting with a stream of wealthy suitors. So what was he going to do about it?

Not a thing. He didn't have the right. But would he be able to stand back and watch his princess shower her attention on another man? *His princess.* Possessive thoughts about a woman he shouldn't want?

He raked an angry hand through his hair. He didn't deal well with confusion. What goes around, comes around. It was only fitting that she would cause chaos in his life after he'd turned her life upside down. The question remained: What was he going to do about it?

Chapter Eight

On the following Friday night, at quitting time, Alexis was ready for a night out. For a solid two weeks, she had spent her mornings arranging and furnishing her grandmother's new apartment, her afternoons with a voice coach learning to speak "the Queen's English," and her evenings with a French tutor. Apparently, any princess worth her crown had a basic understanding of the French language. At least enough to order from an expensive, pretentious menu. As a reward for her effort, Yanis was taking her to a new, *très chic* restaurant to test her skills.

She had no desire to try out a place where the house specialities were snails, fish eggs, and frog legs. She would, however, accept any invitation that included Nick. He had been busy with other clients and she had only seen him briefly at the studio, with other people always around. Mostly he kept in touch by phone. The few times she had spoken to him he had been polite and professional. She might have been discouraged except he had gone out of his way to talk to her when he really had no business reason.

Several times she had been tempted to take Yanis up on his offer to share his gossip about Nick. But she always stopped herself because she wanted Nick to open up to her on his own. Tonight, she would get some information from him, or she would die trying.

She glanced through her closet at her ever-expanding wardrobe. No matter what she chose, she knew she would look great. Her ego had not gone out of control. Yanis Costas was good at his job. He liked to dress women and he knew how to make the most of their assets. Her hand hovered over a peach colored pantsuit before settling on the red cocktail dress.

In this dress you will be more likely to go after what you want.

She planned to test that theory because she definitely had someone she wanted to go after.

If she couldn't get his attention in this slinky scarlet number, she wouldn't get his attention at all. Even with the more modest length she had talked the designer into, the dress, along with a pair of red stiletto heals, was more daring than anything she'd worn in public in years. At seven o'clock she went downstairs to meet Yanis in the studio.

"You're going to stop hearts in that dress," he said.

"Yeah, right," she muttered.

"Stop mumbling and remember to lose that accent in public. You sound like you belong in the cast of the Sopranos." He tugged at the hem of her dress and the neckline plunged lower. "That's better."

"If I didn't know you better, I'd swear you were interested."

A booming laugh echoed around the room. "You are like my little sister. And I couldn't be more proud of you if we were related. I know you had your reservations about all this but you've adapted beautifully."

She shyly shrugged off the compliment. "It's all in the clothes."

"In public I will proudly take the credit. But between you and me, it's in the genes. The princess might not be who you are, but it's *what you are.*"

Technically he was right, but since childhood, being called a princess had always been an insult rather than a compliment. Rather than seeking attention, she had actively tried to avoid it. She was still overwhelmed by the thought of what lay ahead.

He cupped his hand on her shoulder. "If you don't believe me, ask your other date tonight. He will tell you I'm right."

"And how would you know? Do you guys stand around discussing things like that?"

"I can honestly say that you are not our main topic of conversation. However, you do seem to be the focal point of his attention when you're not looking."

A wave of happiness washed over her. She hoped Yanis was right about Nick's interest.

"And before you go off on me for that comment," Yanis said, "ask yourself if the scenery is what you are focused on when he is in the same room with you." He offered his arm. "Ready?"

"As ready as I'll ever be."

Outside, a black stretch limo waited to take them to the Upper East Side. Labor Day weekend had begun, and the traffic moved at a crawl. The thirty city blocks took almost a half hour to cover. The pure luxury of the car should have been a distraction but she was preoccupied with the thought of seeing Nick. When they finally arrived at the posh restaurant, a line of people were waiting outside, gawking like spectators.

"I hope we have reservations," Alexis mused aloud.

"Better. We have an invitation to the grand opening."

"A grand opening?" she repeated.

"The proceeds go to benefit breast cancer research."

So much for some quiet time with Nick. The place would be a mob scene. She could comfort herself with the knowledge that the cause was worthwhile.

Alexis exited the limo and walked down the cordoned entrance on Yanis' arm. Flashbulbs snapped, blurring her vision. Having gotten to know Yanis on a personal level, she had forgotten that he was something of a celebrity as he played to his crowd. For herself, she had never craved the limelight and the only way for her to get past the curious onlookers was to ignore them completely. She probably came off like a stuck up witch instead of the skittish kitten she felt like.

The doorman opened the etched glass doors

and, once they were safely inside, the *maître d'* greeted them with a polite bow. "Your Highness. Your table is waiting."

Alexis nearly choked. Several heads turned at the formal greeting. Embarrassment brought a hot flush to her cheeks.

"We'd like to keep her identity quiet," Yanis confided softly.

The man nodded discretely but the damage was already done. She shot a glare toward Yanis. Despite his softly spoken words, she had no doubt that her identity was meant to cause a stir. Her reward dinner was looking more like a trial run. She wasn't ready to play the part.

Her stomach knotted as the irony of the situation hit her. She wasn't playing a part. This time she was playing for real. She squared her shoulders and raised her chin higher. If Yanis and Nick wanted a princess, then a princess they would get.

Nick watched Alexis from the bar with mixed feelings. Everything about her screamed class, from her poise to her walk to the way she gracefully lowered herself into the tapestry covered seat of the booth. He couldn't believe the difference in her in just a few short weeks.

Clothes might not make a person, but they did help to foster a certain image. The rest . . . that had to be part of her DNA.

As a normal, red-blooded male with a working libido, he liked what he saw. As a man who knew Alexis before the change, he was torn. Was there anything sexier than the first photograph he had seen of her straddling a motorcycle? That woman was free-spirited and comfortable in her life. Now she was regal and sensual, but sadly subdued. After tonight, it would be too late to turn back.

He strode from the bar to the table. When Alexis caught sight of him her smile became brighter and her eyes sparked a deeper shade of blue. The effect he had on her was more than flattering, it was intoxicating.

"Mr. Lanborne, how wonderful of you to join us." She offered her hand.

He covered her delicate fingers with his and kissed the back of her hand. Her skin felt soft against his lips and it took all his control to let go of her, when he wanted to devour her right then and there. "Princess."

She flinched at the greeting but recovered quickly and beautifully. "Have a seat. We were just discussing the state of the economy."

Yanis chuckled. "Funny. I thought we were

discussing how you couldn't balance your check book when you were an accountant by trade."

"That's the state of my personal economy." Her laugh was engaging and seductive. If she was aware of the attention she had captured in the restaurant, she didn't show it. Even the waiter paused to admire her when he delivered the menus.

As a rule, Nick avoided this kind of event. Try as he did to convince himself that business brought him here, the real reason was the woman seated across from him. "See anything you like on the menu?" he asked.

"I understand the coq au vin is fabulous," Yanis commented.

Alexis scanned the leather bound menu with interest. "Don't they have mozzarella sticks?" she whispered. Her eyes sparkled in the chandelier lighting.

Apparently her sense of humor went past Yanis. "Don't go middle class on me, Princess. If you're in the mood for cheese, have the baked Brie."

When the waiter returned, Alexis left the ordering as well as the bulk of the conversation to Yanis. Instead, she gave her attention to the strolling violin player who serenaded the patrons with a haunting French melody.

Her delicate features were animated but her eyes were hooded, as if she hid a wealth of secrets. What was she thinking?

He had left Yanis to tell her about tonight, but Nick got the distinct impression that the designer hadn't warned her. This would be a baptism by fire. With less than a month left until the launch, they needed to prepare her for what lay ahead. Yanis wanted a venue that would attract enough attention to make the society pages. Nick insisted on an event conservative enough in its guest list to keep the tabloid press away.

Alexis had caused a fair amount of speculation, but who wouldn't be curious about an attractive woman? Even without her title, she would garnish the interest of the men in the room. She had his undivided attention without uttering a single word. Her body language spoke volumes.

Before the appetizers were served, Nick's beeper went off. Since his office staff rarely contacted him, he knew he had to return the call. "I'll be right back."

It took five minute to find a quiet area from which to make a call and another ten minutes to pacify a whining client. His policy of being available twenty-four hours a day to his clientele wasn't often tested, but tonight the intrusion was more of an annoyance than usual. So much for his personal mantra that clients paid the bills and women were nothing but a big expense. He knew where he wanted to be right now, and it wasn't in a darkened hallway taking a business call.

When he finally finished he returned to the lobby. Through the spacious archway, he had a clear view of Alexis. She was gorgeous, and no matter how hard he tried to fight the pull, he was completely drawn to her. He crossed the crowded bar and headed toward the table. The rumble of quiet conversation and mouth-watering aromas hung in the air. Awareness of Alexis' many charms seemed to heighten all his other senses as well.

"Why, Nicholas. This is a surprise."

The words stopped him in his tracks. He knew without looking that the voice belonged to his ex-fiancé. For cold shock, ice water wouldn't have been as effective. Until that moment, he had been enjoying his night out. He turned and nodded his head curtly. "Sharon."

She drew up next to him, champagne glass in hand. "You're looking well."

"Thank you."

He didn't return the compliment. Despite designer clothes, meticulously styled hair, and flawless makeup, she was still just an imitation of a socialite. He hadn't seen her since their split, going as far as to avoid the industry functions she might have attended with his previous boss. Now he wondered why. In hindsight, they had done him a huge favor. He never would have struck out on his own otherwise.

"I hear you're doing very well for yourself, Nick." Her voice, which he had once found so sultry, had no effect on him. Neither did her blatant appraisal.

"I'm managing."

"I'll say. Winning the Cleo Award, landing the Costas account. And rumor has it you're dining with royalty tonight."

He schooled his features. "Do you believe everything you hear?"

"That isn't an answer, Nick." She couldn't hide her curiosity but he wasn't about to clue her in.

"And you didn't ask a question," he countered. "If you'll excuse me . . ."

She took hold of his arm and he couldn't extract himself without causing a scene. "I was on my way over to say hello to Yanis Costas. He used to be our client."

"*Used* to be," he stressed.

"That's no excuse for poor manners," she purred.

He would bet the proverbial farm that Sharon's interest was not in an ex-client, but more in the third party at the table. She wanted to check out the woman who had caused a stir among the staff and male guests alike. Maybe even see if she could cultivate an association she could later exploit.

She hadn't changed. But had he? He had actively gone after the Costas account to get back at the two people who had wronged him. If he was honest with himself, he'd admit that his relationship had been over long before she left for a bigger fish. She had wanted more than he was able to give. His pride had been hurt, not his heart. But his determination to win at any cost made him no better than Sharon. He had gotten what he wanted. Too bad Alexis would be the one who paid the real price for his wounded pride.

"Oh, now this should be interesting," Yanis said. "How are you in a cat fight?"

Alexis followed Yanis' gaze to the striking blond who had cornered Nick on the way back to the table. Her possessive stance and demonstrative gestures were not those of a stranger. What kind of prior relationship did they have? Not that it was any of her business, but that didn't stop her stomach from twisting into a painful knot when the other woman touched Nick. Feeling jealous and insecure—and hating the emotion—she gave her attention back to Yanis. "Do you know her?"

He loosened the collar at his throat. "Quite well. Her name is Sharon Harrison, once the fiancé of Nick Lanborne, and currently married to Nick's old boss."

"What?" she choked out.

"Nick never told you about her?"

Nick never mentioned that there was an *ex* let alone talked about her. She shouldn't be surprised. He hadn't reached the age of thirty without a relationship or two in his past. The way the woman clung to him as they came toward the table made Alexis wonder if she wanted to become the current woman on Nick's arm.

Her appetite was officially ruined. She wouldn't be able to swallow past the lump in her throat. She wasn't even sure she would be able to rise to her feet for an introduction. As she tried, Yanis placed a restraining hand on her leg.

He leaned in closer. "Royalty never stands for the commoners."

Turbulent emotions aside, she couldn't help but smile. "Thank you."

Despite the lack of fabric used in her dress,

the clothing did act as a shield. She looked good, even if butterflies were dancing in her stomach. Competition never bothered her but comparison did. If this woman represented Nick's taste, Alexis didn't stand a chance.

"Yanis, how good to see you again. We've missed you since you left us." Sharon's voice lilted with a sexy sigh.

Yanis came to his feet and accepted her outstretched hand. "Life goes on."

"I guess that's just the nature of the advertising business."

"Oh, yes, there is a lot of bed-hopping in this business, figuratively speaking, of course."

Alexis nearly choked on her Perrier.

Sharon's smile barely faltered, but her eyes narrowed as she glanced toward Alexis. "Yes, well I just stopped over to pay my respects."

Yanis tipped his head. "How thoughtful. Send my regards to your husband."

Sharon paused, as if she was waiting for an introduction. Before either man could speak, the waiter arrived with the appetizers and she was forced to step aside to let the man through. Nick extracted himself from her grip and slid into the booth while she walked back to her friends.

Alexis didn't know whether to feel relieved

or insulted at the lack of an introduction. She wasn't up to putting on royal airs for Nick's ex, a woman who obviously set the bar for how all other women were now judged by him. At the same time, she wondered if the slight had been deliberate. If so, why? One part of his past had been revealed, but that left her with a whole new set of questions. Number one being, why did that woman keep glancing over at their table when she had dinner companions of her own? Did she realize what a huge mistake she'd made in giving up a man like Nick?

Nick's earlier good mood had evaporated, replaced with a quiet tension. Did he still hold feelings for his elegant ex-fiancé? Why else would her presence have caused an about-face in his mood?

Before the main course was even placed on the table, Alexis was ready to leave. Yanis' lighthearted banter was wasted on her. She smiled and laughed at the appropriate times, but her heart wasn't in it. It was going to be a long night.

"Would you care to see the Viennese table?" the waiter asked when their plates were cleared.

"I couldn't eat another bite," Alexis said, although she had eaten relatively little. She didn't want anything that would prolong the agony of this evening.

"First, I have a little surprise for you, then we can leave," Yanis promised.

"The mind reels that there could be more excitement tonight," she said dryly. She glanced toward Nick. At least she could make him smile, even if she hadn't gotten a word out of him.

Yanis took hold of her arm and escorted her from the main dining hall. "I guess I should tell you that you made a very generous contribution for breast cancer research."

"I did?"

"Yes and the local representative wants to thank you personally."

If it would move her closer to the door, she would go along. She met the representative in a banquet hall that held a photographer poised for a photo op. She looked around for Nick, but he had taken a different exit. Had he left without saying good-bye? She had a hard time striking a joyous pose with Yanis when her heart was on her sleeve and her spirits had taken a nosedive. Finally they were out the door and she would soon be on her way home. The limo was waiting by the curb.

Inside the spacious car, Nick was already

seated. She exhaled in relief. He hadn't deserted her.

The driver pulled around the corner and
stopped two blocks up the road. Yanis took
Alexis' hand. "You were magnificent, Lexie.
Didn't everything go perfectly, Nick?"

"Perfectly," he agreed, although his expression didn't hold much conviction.

"This is just the first of what I'm sure will
be many interesting nights," Yanis added.
"This is my stop. The car is yours for the rest
of the night." He kissed the back of her hand
then whispered, "Make the most of that red
dress, darling."

Heat infused her cheeks. Earlier in the evening, she might have done just that. That had
been her plan all along. Now, Nick looked as
if he was ready for a quick escape himself.

So far, the day had been a total bust. If they
parted now, all that would remain would be a
lot of bad memories. No way did she want this
to be his lasting impression of the night. She
didn't usually require a brick to the head
before she gave up on a man, but she couldn't
forget the kiss they'd shared in her apartment.
He had wanted her as much as she'd wanted
him. Those feelings didn't just disappear.
They got buried under a pile of old baggage.

She had spent the last two weeks, not to mention the better part of the evening, trying to fit into a world that wasn't her own. This wasn't the real Alexis. If he was going to judge her against another woman, she wanted to make sure he was making the right comparison. She had seen him in his element. It was time he saw her in hers.

Chapter Nine

Nick stretched his legs out in the spacious backseat. What a night! Thankfully, it was almost over. He stared out the tinted window. Anything was better than focusing on the stunning woman seated next to him. He tried, but couldn't block out the alluring scent of her or close his mind to the warmth of her body close to his. When had his mind ceded power to his hormones? The sooner he saw Alexis to her door the safer he would be.

"Should I have the driver take you home?"

"No."

"No?" he repeated, surprised, but he should have known she wouldn't make this easy on him.

"Yanis said the car was mine for the night."

"What did you have in mind?"

"It's early. I think I'll head over to Brooklyn."

He clenched his hands into tight fists. "You shouldn't be going over there alone at this time of night."

She smiled. "Then come with me."

"I don't think so."

Alexis shrugged. "Suit yourself. I've got my very own designated driver, so I think I'd like to hit a few bars." She reached behind and pulled the pins that held her chignon in place. Silky brown waves framed her face. She shook her head, freeing the hair. The effect was a tousled look that transformed her from cool socialite to beautiful siren.

No way would he let her go club-hopping in her old neighborhood looking like that! Not without an escort. She might not be looking for trouble, but trouble sure would find her. Didn't she realize the effect she had on men?

"I suppose I could go for a couple of hours."

"Don't torture yourself, Nick. I wouldn't want you to do anything out of character, like loosen up and have fun."

"I said I was going with you."

"As you like," she said with a slight shrug of her shoulders.

She made him sound about as appealing as warm milk. So why did he get the feeling he had just been manipulated into going with her? Wouldn't she have preferred to fly solo and meet a more exciting man?

Over his dead body!

"Where in Brooklyn?" he asked. He'd deal with the consequences of this fool-hearted outing later.

"Flatbush. I know a great place."

"I'll bet you do." He gave the limo driver the instructions and braced himself for a bumpy ride tonight.

"By the way, Nick, have you ever ridden on a mechanical bull?"

Nick thought she was joking until they arrived at their destination. The Silver Spur was a country-western restaurant and saloon. It touted itself as "a little bit of Texas in New York" and he could see why. He glanced at the oak bar and the western paraphernalia on the walls. Inhaling, he smelled a mix of grilled meat and beer.

The place was filled to capacity with what Alexis had affectionately referred to as week-end cowboys. They were overdressed for the jeans and western boots set that frequented the establishment. A fact the familiar waitress felt the need to point out as she made their drinks at the bar.

"Did you mug a penguin on the way here?" Marissa asked.

Nick slid his arm across Alexis' back and led her toward an empty table. "Tell me again why you thought I would enjoy this."

"I never said you'd enjoy it, I just thought you could see how the other half lives."

"What other half?"

She sat in a wooden chair and he took the seat next to her. She waved to several people before giving her undivided attention to him. "The people who let go and don't give a flying fig what anyone thinks about them. The people you see for exactly who they are, and you like them anyway."

Nick tossed a quick glance at the crowd circling the mechanical bull and hooting for the poor sap on top. "Oh. That other half. Because the half with self-control and restraint apparently have a problem."

"Not in every situation. Only when they use it to shut people out of their lives."

"Which is apparently how you view me."

She took a sip of her drink, then ran her tongue over her ruby lips with a sigh. "I can't figure you out. Sometimes you just can't help yourself, and a little bit of the real you jumps out, but you fight it. It makes me wonder why."

"Do you devote a lot of time wondering about me?" he asked with a chuckle.

"It's a great way to pass the time between fittings." She gave him an appreciative once-over and grinned. "But don't worry, I'm learning to think about you without my Brooklyn accent so my time's not totally wasted."

"It's comforting to know that I'm being dissected in the Queen's English."

"Do you mean to tell me that you don't think about me? I'm crushed."

Oh, he thought about her. More than he should and in ways that he shouldn't. And right about now, he was thinking how he wanted to get out of there and take her somewhere to show her what he was like when he let loose. She knew just how to push his buttons, both literally and figuratively.

"So you hope to see a different side of me if I give a try to that bucking pile of metal?"

"The only side of you I'd see is your backside. It's not as easy as it looks."

"Then what's the point?"

Alexis shook her head. "I doubt you would understand."

"Try me, anyway."

As she leaned in closer, her leg brushed against his. A breath caught in her throat and she uttered a soft groan that echoed right through him. For a brief second she closed her eyes and purred like a contented kitten. She was entranced in her own private thoughts, yet she held him spellbound. He felt like a voyeur intruding on an intimate moment.

The vocal tirade of one more urban cowboy who had hit the floor mat brought her back to reality. Her eyes fluttered open and she quickly took in her surroundings. He could almost see her blush despite the muted lighting. She folded her arms across her chest. When she lifted her gaze she caught him staring at her indiscretely.

"You were saying?" Nick said.

"I was?"

"Why we're here."

"Everyday, I feel like I'm losing a little part of me. I'm not ready to let go of it all."

"And what does this place have to do with it?"

"This is where I feel comfortable. I used to work here on weekends and a lot of my friends hang out here."

He realized that he knew very little about her old life despite all the information he had gathered. But, surprisingly, he wanted to know her better. Judging solely on her dossier, she had been a single working girl with a moderate income and no major commitments, either financial or personal. Alexis was a prime example of where the cold facts didn't add up to the whole picture.

What he couldn't figure out was why she wanted to include him in the one part of her life she fought to hold onto. Wasn't he responsible for everything she felt she was losing? Any other woman and he might have thought guilt was the motive. Not with Alexis. She seemed genuinely happy to share this with him.

As the night progressed he began to see a side of her he'd never seen before. That wasn't true—this was the woman in the first photograph he'd seen. The sassy, motorcycling free spirit who had caught his attention and refused to let go. She knew how to take care of herself, but not for one moment did he get the impression she was out for herself.

Lexie Marks was a woman of many passions. She loved to talk, she loved to laugh, and she loved life. More unsettling was the realization that he liked the way he felt when he was with her. That was something he'd never experienced with another woman.

He sat back in his chair and watched her move on the dance floor. She wasn't hard to spot since she was the only woman doing the country line dance in a red cocktail dress. Her high heel shoes had been discarded after the first dance and her stocking-clad feet slid gracefully on the highly polished wood floors. She was a sight, and he couldn't take his eyes off her.

He knew he should clear out before he got in any deeper. His reasons for keeping their relationship strictly professional hadn't changed. But his feelings had. The woman had waged a war for his heart. Somehow, she had found a way to breach his highly developed defenses and she was able to walk in whenever she wanted. All the more reason to put some distance between himself and this sexy opponent. So why did he stay in the enemy camp?

Alexis noticed Nick observing her on the dance floor. His gaze never strayed. Although she usually preferred not to be the center of attention, she did like being his main attraction. She hoped his interest was more than a businessman looking out for his investment, but with Nick, it was hard to tell. His mood had improved dramatically since leaving the restaurant. She couldn't help but wonder, however, if his ex-fiancé was still on his mind.

"I'm wiped," she said as she fell into the chair next to him. She took a sip of her drink to cool her thirst, but she had a hunger no amount of tonic water could fill.

Lord, he looked good in black. Although he would probably look good in anything. She swallowed hard. Her blatant musings regarding the man were hardly refined or aristocratic, but as long as she still controlled her own thoughts, he would be center stage.

"Let me get the check and we'll go," he said.

"There's no check. It's on the house tonight."

"It pays to have friends," he quipped and dropped a large tip on the table.

They left the noisy bar just after midnight. The night air felt cool over her bare shoulders. Despite the late hour, the streets were fairly crowded in the city that never slept. They waited on the sidewalk for the driver to pull the car around.

"I'll take you back to your apartment now." Nick draped his arm across her shoulders. His warmth gave her a sense of peace she didn't want to lose.

"I'm not going back there tonight." She might not get what she wanted from him but she wasn't about to return to her lonely apartment and obsess about it.

"Where did you plan to go?"

She hadn't made any plans but she was reluctant to end the evening. "Maybe I'll go back inside and wait for Marissa to get off." She glanced at her watch. "That's only two more hours."

"I thought you were tired."

"I've been more tired than this and worked a full shift behind the bar. Or maybe I'll just drive around all night in the back of the limo."

Deep lines etched in his face expressed his disapproval. "That doesn't sound like a very good idea."

"Do you have any ideas in mind?" she challenged.

"What could be better than your Fifth Avenue apartment?"

"Since it's not mine, anywhere is a better place to be."

"Even my place?"

"Now that you mention it . . . especially your place."

He groaned in disbelief.

"Is that so inconceivable?" she asked. Nick's home would be a reflection of the real him. Naturally, she was curious.

"I think maybe you've had one too many and you're not thinking clearly, Lexie."

Did he realize he had used her nickname?

He had always been so formal with her. "I am not tipsy, if that's what you're worried about."

His eyebrow arched skeptically.

She raised up on her toes and brushed a kiss over his mouth, lingering long enough to make sure he tasted her. Long enough to get a taste of him. The physical attraction was there. Why was he still holding back? She could only think of one reason.

"No alcohol has touched these lips tonight. If I am intoxicated, then it is from something you do to me, not from something I drank."

They strolled slowly along the block. "I am not the kind of man you want to get involved with."

"I'm an adult, Nick. I do know what I want. Maybe I'm not the kind of woman you want to get involved with and I can accept that. I admit, I'm not at all like your ex-fiancé . . ."

He stopped in his tracks, taking hold of her arm. "Wait a second. What does she have to do with anything?"

"I don't know. But you didn't seem all that indifferent to me before she waltzed over to the table tonight. And since I didn't rate an introduction, I figure there must be some unfinished business between you."

The limo pulled up to the curb. When Alexis

didn't make a move toward the vehicle, he turned to face her. "Let me get a few things straight for you. There is *no* unfinished business regarding my ex, *she* did not rate an introduction to *you*, and the last thing I feel about you is indifference. That should be reason enough for you to stay away if you had any sense."

"Does that mean you're taking me to see your home?" Her voice quivered, but her smile was pure triumph.

"Do I have a choice?"

"You always have a choice, Nick."

"That's what you think, Princess." If she had gotten to him at last, then it was only fair. Her mind had long ago ceded power to her body. Her heart was quickly following. The least she could do was bring him along for the ride.

What had he been thinking? Nick's loft apartment in Soho was his last bastion of solitude. He had moved to the city after his ex left. From the time he struck out on his own he had put all his time, money, and energy into his business. His office was his showcase. His apartment was a place he went to disconnect.

He perched on the daybed and watched Alexis inspect his home. She walked between the open rooms, pausing long enough to give attention to sparse surroundings. The comfortable, functional furniture suited him. He had never given much thought to the decor. He'd never needed to, since this was his own private sanctuary. Oddly, she seemed to fit right in.

He took in her entire appearance. She had discarded her shoes upon arrival. Her hair, wild from an evening of dancing framed her face, flushed with excitement.

"It's not what I expected, Nick."

"What did you expect?"

The hem of her skirt swirled around her legs as she spun toward him. "I guess something a bit more like your public persona. You see, I knew there was another side to you."

He had never thought of himself as having another persona. He had become so used to keeping a cool, detached distance from people, it had become a natural way of life. Was that why he never changed his apartment, even after he could afford to? Was he holding on to a part of himself, the same way Alexis fought so hard to do?

She sat next to him on the edge of the bed. Close enough to feel her heat, close enough to smell her feminine scent. "Anyway, I really like it here."

He shook his head in disbelief. "It hardly

compares to yours."

"I don't know. Yours has some definite advantages."

"Name one."

Alexis smiled broadly. "You're here." She turned and looked out the window at the sparkling city lights. The top of the Empire State Building was lit in red, white, and blue in honor of Labor Day weekend. Did the city look exceptionally spectacular tonight, or was she just feeling that way?

She pivoted around and glanced at the bed. Her pulse fluttered. He was so gorgeous. She would have been put off by his silence, except she had no idea what to say either. If she followed her heart, she would be spouting sonnets. Somehow, she didn't think he was ready for that. She had just gotten him past the major hurdle of seeing her as a real woman instead of an investment he needed to protect.

"Do you have any plans for the weekend?" she asked.

He chuckled and it warmed her in all the right places. "It's a little late to be asking since you're here."

"You could have said no."

Nick raised his head and cast her a dubious glance. "Is that so?"

She shrugged and slowly strolled around the

bedroom. One wall had built-in book shelves and was filled with quite a collection. Classics, work related nonfiction as well as best sellers lined the wall. Stuck in between two volumes of Dickens sat a Cleo Award, half hidden by shadows. The only television in his apartment was a portable one perched on a shelf. It told her a lot about how he spent his down time. She also learned a lot about Nick himself. Smart, successful, and unpretentious. He wasn't driven by money, but he was certainly driven.

She wandered in front of his desk. The solid teakwood surface reflected the track lighting. When she crossed in front, the glare lifted from the desk, and she noticed a picture of her on top of it. Not one she had posed for in the studio, but a candid shot of her on Marissa's Harley. Lexie Marks as she used to be. Her stomach clenched painfully. She didn't feel like that person anymore. And she had sworn to herself that she wouldn't change inside.

She held up the photograph. "Where did you get this?"

He eased off the bed and walked toward her. "The private investigator I hired to find you."

"Oh."

"You've changed since then."

"I guess so." A cool chill blew over her.

Although he probably thought he was paying her a compliment, his words stung. Would the woman in the photograph have captured his interest?

"Are you angry?"

"About the picture?" She shook her head. "No." She laid it back on the desk.

"Then you're upset about the private investigator."

"I knew about that. You showed me the reports, remember?" How could she explain her confusing emotions when she couldn't figure them out herself? Yes, she was a different person outside, but she was the same person inside. Could he have fallen for the old Lexie, or was he drawn only to the new one? Did it matter as long as she had him? She knew in her heart that it did. Once the campaign ended, she could never live up to the hype.

He draped his arms across her shoulder. "So what's bothering you?"

"Absolutely nothing," she said as she leaned into him. She wasn't going to ruin the remainder of the night with nagging doubts about a situation she couldn't change. She knew the risks going in.

"Are you sure?"

"I was feeling a little cold. I'm better now."

His arms tightened around her. For a man

who admitted that sensitivity was not his strong suit, he had an instinctual way of calming her fears. When he held her, everything felt right.

"You need sleep. Take the bedroom," he said.

Reluctant to let go too soon, she cuddled closer. "The overstuffed sofa in the living room looks fine."

"It isn't comfortable for sleeping."

"Like I might be able to sleep tonight knowing you're right in the next room?" she muttered.

"Then that will make two of us. Next time, be careful what you wish for." He dropped a light kiss on her forehead and left her alone in the bedroom.

With a deep exhale of disappointment, she grabbed a book from the shelf and steeled onto her masculine bed. There was a wall separating them but it beat spending another night alone in her beautiful but sterile apartment.

Chapter Ten

Nick woke the following morning a full two hours later than was customary for him. He had been wrong. The couch wasn't such an uncomfortable place to sleep, if he knew he was giving up his bed for Alexis.

If he wasn't careful, he could get used to this. And he would be a fool. He thought about the Pygmalian irony of their relationship. After knowing a woman as warm and giving as Alexis, cool and aristocratically aloof held no appeal to him. The more he changed her to the perfect female ideal, the more he would lose the woman who had captivated him.

His stomach clenched as if he'd been sucker

punched. If he wasn't careful he would fall in love against his will, despite past experiences and a conscious effort to stay ambivalent.

His gaze turned toward the bedroom. Seeing her curled up on the bed was too much of a distraction for a man who already wasn't thinking clearly. He wandered into the kitchen to put on a pot of coffee. Out of sight, but not out of mind.

When he returned to the living room minutes later, Alexis was emerging from the bathroom.

"Good morning . . . I think," he noted carefully. Dressed in one of his white shirts and her face scrubbed clean of last night's makeup, she was a vision. A vision with an attitude, he discovered when she shot him an angry scowl.

"Don't talk to me before coffee," she warned.

"Should I pour you a cup or just inject it right into your veins?"

"Whichever is quicker," she muttered. "Everything hurts."

He couldn't hold back a laugh, despite her less than happy mood. Even at her worst she was a delight. "You're the one who wanted to go dancing last night."

She trailed her hand over his chest as she passed. "So when can we do this again?"

Before recovering from one night, she was already planning another.

Ten minutes and two cups of java later, she was rejuvenated and letting him know that she did not plan to let him backpedal in their relationship. She curled up next to him in the reclining chair as he read the morning paper.

Normally, he wasn't into togetherness, but her brand of affection didn't bother him. She knew how and when to remain quiet, a trait not common in the women he had dated. Of course, even she had her limits of patience, and when she began to feel neglected, she made her presence known. Before she got too daring, he gripped her wrist and hauled her into his lap.

"Behave."

"What's the point of this royalty thing if I can't do whatever I want?"

He toyed with the collar of the borrowed shirt she wore. "Or take whatever you want. Well, you can't have my shirt." Although he said the words lightly, he was serious. First she would start borrowing his things, then she would be leaving her possessions behind for an excuse to return. Before he knew what was happening he would be in over his head. *Like you aren't already,* he silently mocked himself.

The ring of the phone cut what he was sure would be a flirtatious argument. Alexis expelled a groan of frustration. "Saved by the bell," she said as she handed him the receiver from the coffee table.

He didn't feel saved. Instead, he resented the intrusion. "Hello," he snapped at the caller.

"Have you seen the 'On the Town' column in the *Examiner* yet?" Yanis gushed with annoying cheer.

"I was just getting to it now."

"Our girl has them talking and people were impressed."

From a business standpoint, the objective had been met. The product had survived the first test market. Only she wasn't a product, she was a woman, complicated and emotional.

"That's what you wanted, right?" Nick replied, feeling strangely indifferent to the news.

"Something wrong, Nick?"

"No."

"Oh, then my timing was bad," Yanis noted humorously. "Say hello to Lexie and I'll see you at the studio on Tuesday."

He neither confirmed nor denied Costas' comment. Some subjects were off limits no matter what their professional ties. "Yanis says hello," Nick said after he hung up.

"He called for that?" she asked.

"No. Just a second."

He scanned the pages of the *Examiner* until he came across a small black and white photograph of Alexis and Costas. The caption read, "The Princess and the Fashion King." Nick read the small paragraph below.

"International designer to the elite, Yanis Costas, attended the opening of La Masquerade last night with a mysterious woman at his side. Despite efforts to keep her identity quiet, this reporter learned that the woman was Princess Alexis Markova. The American-born princess is said to be the inspiration for a product line from the House of Yanis. And she was certainly *inspiring* in a flaming red Costas original. Stay tuned. I'm sure we'll be seeing more of the princess in the future."

He folded the paper over and handed it to Alexis, face up. "Here are your first fifteen minutes of fame."

She scanned the small news item. Her reaction was swift and completely unexpected. She dropped the paper on the floor and sprung to her feet. An angry expletive uttered in her Brooklyn accent burst forth from her soft lips.

"What's wrong?"

"I have to go." She darted from the living room.

He caught up with her in the bedroom as she was about to start changing. "Do you want to tell me what's wrong? There was nothing unflattering in that article."

"It's not the article and it's not your problem." When her gaze locked on his, he realized that she wasn't angry, she was worried. And strangely, sad. Didn't she know this day would come?

He took her hands in his. "I'm making it my problem."

"I haven't told my grandmother about the campaign yet. I didn't think I would have to so soon. She was just beginning to respond to the new medication and I wanted to wait until she was completely well."

"Then don't mention it yet."

"There were only two things my grandmother truly loved: playing bridge and reading the society pages with afternoon tea. She's not quite up for bridge yet, but the society pages . . . I need to tell her before she sees it in the paper, or worse, before someone else shows it to her."

"Then I'll go with you."

"You don't have to."

"I want to." He owed her that much. She wasn't the only descendent of European royalty he had considered for the campaign, but the moment he saw her picture, she was the one he had actively pursued. If he hadn't used her title for personal gain he wouldn't have this gnawing sense of remorse. He also wouldn't be so emotionally vested. There was justice in the world, however poetic.

Alexis carried a tray holding a freshly brewed pot of tea into the living room and joined her grandmother on the colonial sofa. The subsidized senior housing complex was bright and airy, and much more modern than their old Brooklyn brownstone. After years of lousy water pressure, loud neighbors, and fighting for heat, Nana deserved this. But was Alexis truly happy for her grandmother or looking to justify her own actions? Nana's health had improved in small increments and her spirits were high. She was dressed in a beige slacks set with a crocheted shawl draped over her shoulders. A definite improvement over the hospital gown. She wasn't quite back to her old self yet, but she was certainly lucid. Still, she never once asked why she had been moved from her home of more than thirty years.

Despite visits three times a week and daily phone calls, Alexis had always found a reason to keep her grandmother in the dark about her work. With the story in the morning papers, Alexis' excuses had run out. Nick had offered to help her explain, but she declined. This was something she had to do alone. Instead, she sent him over to Brooklyn to pick up breakfast at her grandmother's favorite Bavarian bakery.

"You look tired, Lexie. Are you getting enough sleep?"

She rolled her shoulders in a guilty shrug. "Usually. But not last night."

"Maybe you should take a little nap." In her grandmother's eyes, she was still a child.

"How come you never asked why I moved you here?" She poured a cup of tea and handed it to Nana, then poured another for herself.

"I know why."

"You do?" She had trouble swallowing the hot brew over the lump in her throat. Had her grandmother discovered the truth?

"I was ill for a while," Nana said. "With you working two jobs, you couldn't look after me. And I would never expect you to."

If that was what the administration of the facility led her to believe, then Alexis was grateful. "There's more to it than that. I need to tell you something, but please don't be angry with me."

Nana clasped her frail hand over Alexis'. "I could never be angry with you."

She took a manila folder from her oversized purse. She hadn't looked through the papers since the night Nick gave them to her. The collection of old history was something she hadn't wanted to dwell on. She had no choice now.

"I need to show you something."

She handed over the file. As her grandmother slowly leafed though the pages, she could see the pain and sorrow etched into the deep lines on Nana's weathered face. The leap from palace princess to refugee to war widow to working mother and finally guardian grandmother showed the procession of a life lost in small, painful steps. A part of Alexis had always hoped the reports were wrong or inaccurate. No one deserved so much loss in one lifetime.

When she finished reading, Nana closed the file.

"Is it true?" Alexis asked.

Nana tipped her head. "Yes."

"Why didn't you tell me?"

Her eyes clouded in regret. She blinked back the tears that threatened to fall. "I was told never to tell anyone or the revolutionary guards would kill me too. Those are powerfully frightening words to a child."

"Yes they are," Alexis agreed.

"When I escaped to Paris with my great-aunt, she forbade me to ever speak about it. And I never did." The old woman shuddered. She inhaled deeply and regained her composure. "Once, when you were just a baby, a historian came nosing around. I was still too scared to answer questions so I told him he had the wrong woman. Unfortunately, he had talked to some of the neighbors too, looking for verification and it left us the mark for some rather cruel jokes in the neighborhood."

Alexis wiped at a salty tear streaming down her face. "How did you survive it all?"

Nana's expression softened. "What you've read is incomplete, Lexie. It shows only the sadness. It doesn't show the time I had with my parents before they were killed. Or the happiness I had with my husband before the war took him. Nowhere in this report does it show the pure joy your mother and you have given my life. Those are not in any history book, they're in my heart." She handed the folder back to Alexis. "Where did you get this?"

The knot in her stomach clenched tighter. "When you were ill, I was really worried about what would happen to you and I did something . . . I needed money for the nursing home . . . you see it all started with this man . . . Nick Lanborne . . . well, it probably started with Yanis Costas . . . but Nick was the one with the idea . . . and when he came to the house and you were so ill . . . well, Nick sort of offered a solution to my problem . . ." She paused for a breath. She was rambling. In her hurry to get it out, the right words wouldn't come.

"You're not making one bit of sense. The only thing I can tell so far is that your eyes brighten every time you mention this Nick. Is he your beau?"

"No . . . I mean maybe, I'm not sure . . . but I'm trying to tell you something."

"And making a mess of it, Lexie. I know I'm still a bit muddled, but you are losing me."

She exhaled slowly and collected her thoughts. "They wanted to use my title and my face in an ad campaign for a new perfume called Royal Blue. They offered me a lot of money. I didn't know what else to do, and I couldn't ask you . . ." her words trailed off.

A long silence stretched. "And?" Nana finally said.

"And what? That's it. I sold out your secret for money."

Nana touched her trembling hand to Alexis' cheek. "If someone was able to dig up all this information and track you down, then it was not a secret, was it?"

"Well, no, I guess not."

"And you did not sell out for money, you made a deal to help me. Do you believe I would ever hold that against you?"

"No, but unfortunately the secret is out to more than a few stodgy historians." Alexis handed over the newspaper clipping from her pocket.

Nana read the article with true pride. "You went back to the family name. I couldn't be more happy."

"Really?" Alexis' voice peaked with surprise and relief. She had been so afraid of the pain her actions might have caused.

"I have something for you. You might need it." Nana shuffled across the plush carpet to the bookcase and removed a small wooden box. Alexis had seen the box since childhood, but until her grandmother opened it and removed a false bottom, she had never known it held anything. Nana removed a velvet pouch. The older woman's fingers still had a slight tremble as she handed the contents to Alexis. "I've been hiding it for years."

A stunning, teardrop-shaped necklace was adorned in sapphires on one side and engraved with the family coat of arms on the other. "It's magnificent."

"It's a locket, Lexie. Open it."

She did as she was told. Inside were two tiny pictures.

"My parents. Your great-grandparents," Nana said. "My mother sewed that into the liner of my coat before I was sent from the palace so that I would always remember her. That's my last memory of my homeland."

"You should keep it," Alexis said, handing it back.

Nana refused. "I've got a few other small pieces. But this one is your key to the past. Why shouldn't you use it to proudly claim your heritage? My only regret was that I had been too afraid to give your mother the same opportunity."

"I think Mama was happy being the Queen of Flatbush in her time. And she had a good life with Dad. Too short, but full."

Nana nodded. "And now it's your turn to

have a good life, Lexie. Tell me about this Nick fellow. Is he special?"

Tension faded as a ribbon of warmth rippled through her. "Yes."

"And what does he do?"

"He's in advertising."

"I hope he's not the one responsible for those commercials for feminine hygiene products they show on late night television. Because I could do without those."

Alexis shared a laugh with her grandmother for the first time in a long time. "I don't think those are his."

Somehow she didn't see Nick as the type who would even discuss feminine products let alone write ad copy for them. She was still trying to get him out of the middle ages where women were concerned. He saw only two types—women out for themselves or women out of his league. He had pegged her as the former, and by the time he realized he was wrong, she had become the latter.

Yes, she was descended from royalty. That and three dollars would get her a cup of coffee at Starbuck's. The only men who would be impressed by a title were the kind who didn't interest her. While she had made headway with Nick last night, he was still holding back.

Would she ever be able to break through his defenses entirely?

Nana cleared her throat. "Can I assume from that color on your cheeks there is more than business between the two of you?"

Alexis feigned shock. "Didn't you teach me that a lady never tells?"

Nana's gaze scanned the newspaper clipping again. "And this man in the photograph?"

"Yanis Costas, the designer."

"And Nick, he isn't upset that you go out with another man?"

Alexis smiled. "I can honestly say he doesn't feel threatened. Besides, he was with us last night. He just skipped out of the photography session."

Nana relaxed against the couch pillows and took a sip of tea. "When am I going to meet him?"

"Just as soon as he gets back from the bakery at Brighton Beach."

She waved a scolding finger in Alexis' face. "How could you be so mean as to send him there on a Saturday morning? He'll be lucky if he's back before lunchtime. He must really care about you."

She only wished her grandmother was right. She knew he felt obligated toward her, and even felt guilty about the whole arrangement when he discovered why she had accepted the deal. But did he actually care about her? As much as he was capable, she supposed. She didn't know if it was enough to build a future on.

Chapter Eleven

Nick slammed the car door with a grunt. Stubborn, vindictive brat! A quick run to the bakery? Alexis had conveniently forgotten to mention that the local streets were closed to traffic on Saturdays. He had to park a mile away and find a small store in an area of the city unfamiliar to him. He should have listened when she declined his offer of a ride. He could be at home getting some work done instead of chasing down foods called *Babka, Peffernusse* and *Gugelhopf*. Although the aroma that filled the car on the ride back whet his appetite, it did nothing to curb his intense desire to toss Alexis into the East River.

And he knew the minute he saw her smile,

his anger would dissipate. She had wanted to speak to her grandmother alone, he couldn't fault her for that. He worried though how the older Markova would react to the news. Nick had no fear that Alexis would honor her commitment, but without the blessing of the dowager princess, she might lose that spark of fire that made her unique.

He grabbed the bakery boxes from the passenger seat and strode the last block to the apartment complex. He shared the elevator with several septuagenarian women who had more than a passing interest in his selection of sweets. At least that's what he chose to believe when they commented on his delicious buns. Either that, or he had been propositioned by Grandma Moses and her cohorts. He was relieved when he arrived on the ninth floor and he could make a quick exit. At the end of the long corridor he found the apartment he wanted and rang the bell.

When the door opened, he came face to face with Nadianna Markova. For a woman in her seventies, she appeared stately, if somewhat tired.

"Mr. Lanborne?" Her clear voice still held the trace of a European accent.

"Yes, Your Highness," he said with a slight bow over the boxes in his hands.

The corners of her mouth lifted in a smile. "No one has called me that in more than half a century."

"I've been told it is the correct way to address you."

"Do you address my granddaughter in this manner, too?"

He tipped his head. "Sometimes."

Her eyebrow arched in question. "And she lets you get away with it?"

"Never," he said with a chuckle. Alexis had her own subtle forms of revenge.

"I thought not." She stepped aside to allow him to enter.

Evidently the older Markova knew the younger one very well. He shouldn't be surprised, but family dynamics, at least those that worked, always amazed him. His family had consisted of a mother he rarely saw and a father he had never known, despite living in the same house with the old man. He knew more about Alexis' family history than his own. His conscience mocked him. He knew her past because he had a professional purpose for searching. His general rule with women had always been the less he knew the easier it would be to walk away. Whatever his reasons in the beginning, the fact remained that he did know the truth now, and it had brought him closer to Alexis than he had ever been with another person.

"Where would you like me to put these boxes?" he asked.

"The kitchen table will be fine. And I apologize for Lexie's behavior. Sending you to the old neighborhood on Saturday was just plain cruel."

"I'll take it up with her."

"If you are brave enough to wake her . . ."

His gaze traveled to the living room where Alexis was sprawled across the sofa. He might be brave enough, but he wasn't crazy. The woman was dangerous when sleep deprived, and he wanted to keep the current arrangement of his limbs intact. He'd pass on the chance to wake sleeping beauty. A fresh pot of coffee brewing in the kitchen accomplished the deed for him. With a languishing stretch and a small yawn, she awoke to the aroma.

She walked into the kitchen, rubbing the sleep from her eyes. "Took you long enough."

"I wonder why," he grumbled.

"Because you're a man and therefore wouldn't stop for directions?"

Her grandmother sighed and took her to task. "Lexie! Is that how I taught you to treat a guest?"

"No," she muttered, pretending to be contrite, but Nick wasn't fooled. She didn't have an ounce of remorse.

He chuckled. "She's still working on refining her genteel manners and aristocratic diplomacy."

"Don't expect miracles. You can take the girl out of Brooklyn, but you can't take Brooklyn out of the girl," Alexis said.

Despite her declaration to the contrary, Nick noticed a change in her. Over coffee, they listened as the older Markova confirmed what he already knew to be true. Only the truth was so much more poignant than the fact sheets and it had affected Alexis deeply. Before today, she had never fully allowed herself to believe, as if she had been hired to play the part of a fairy tale princess, not be herself. As her grandmother spoke, her fingers kept playing over the necklace at her throat. The teardrop shaped heirloom had been prophetic in light of its history.

Nick viewed the breakthrough with mixed emotions. From one side, Alexis would be more at ease with her role now that she was sure of her lineage. A compliant princess made for a satisfied client. He should be proud. He had accomplished his goal. So why did he have an empty feeling eating away at his gut? This morning he had almost allowed himself to think about a future with her. Now he felt as if he had reached the beginning of the end.

Alexis looked though her closet. Her first impulse had been to reach for something from her old wardrobe. Instead, she picked a two-piece suit in a pale peach linen. Very elegant and conservative. Completely unlike her usual taste. She had to stop fighting the process. She had made a commitment to Yanis and Nick, and she also owed it to her grandmother to honor the Markova name. Like it or not, every time she appeared in public, she had to project a royal image. She would just limit the time she spent in public.

However, she wasn't about to turn down a dinner invitation with Nick, even if it meant playing her part. Afterward, she would get him alone and she could be herself again. Her biggest fear was that he would mix up her public persona with her private one.

After leaving her grandmother that afternoon, he had been decidedly quiet and reserved. Nana's revelations couldn't have come as a shock to him since he had known the truth before Alexis. As she styled her hair and applied her makeup, she tried to figure out the puzzle that was Nick. What was going through his mind? Getting him to talk about himself was like pulling teeth. He was a master of evasion.

When the doorbell rang ten minutes later, her musings came to an end. She sprinted from the bedroom to answer. Nick stood on her doorstep, keys in hand, looking sexy and comfortable in his jeans and cotton pullover. The first time he stepped out of character and went for the casual look, she had to be decked out in her designer original. They couldn't get on the same page.

"Are you ready?" he asked, as if he didn't notice their clashing styles.

"Well, one of us is dressed inappropriately," she grumbled. "Let me go change."

"What you have on is . . ." He cleared his throat. "Well, suffice it to say that you look good. And anything you choose to wear is appropriate where we're going."

"Where would that be?"

"You'll see."

Normally she enjoyed surprises, but she'd had more than enough of them the past month. Nick had been the one constant. Was he going to start changing like everything else in her life?

Being his usual, closed-mouth self, he volunteered no information on the car ride out of the city. She braced herself for a long, silent trip but they arrived at their destination in a quarter of an hour. Where they were, however, was a mystery. A deserted parking lot in the middle of nowhere.

"We're here," he announced as he cut the engine.

"We are?" She scanned the area. Not a restaurant in sight. And when Nick took a large paper sack from the trunk of his car she realized she wasn't going to find one. An evening picnic? He hadn't stepped out of character, he had taken a flying leap.

Walking in heels across the grassy path to the picnic area was a slow and precise process. The wobbly hike was worth the effort. Lookout Point along the New Jersey Palisades was not what she had expected when she dressed for dinner, and she wouldn't have traded it for a five star restaurant. The top of the rocky cliffs afforded a stunning view of the New York skyline. A wrought-iron fence was the only thing that stood between them and a sheer drop to the Hudson River below. The balmy summer air and magnificent backdrop were perfect for alfresco dining. Having Nick alone was the icing on the cake.

"How did you ever find this place?" she asked as she sat at the wooden table.

He placed a paper bag on the table and sat on the bench next to her. "I did my last two years of high school in New Jersey. This was *the* place to bring a girl on Saturday nights."

She surveyed the nearly empty park. "Oh, yeah? It doesn't seem to be a hot spot anymore."

"Once it gets dark, it will be mobbed with young lovers."

"I'll take your word on that." She took a plastic tablecloth from the bag and spread it across the table. "So, where did you spend your first years of high school?"

"Excuse me?"

"You said you spent two years in New Jersey. Where were you before that?"

It was as if she was asking him to reveal state secrets. He gave his attention to the bags as if he'd never heard the question. He couldn't avoid her forever. If he didn't want to talk, he shouldn't have taken her to a place where he had her undivided attention.

He continued his task as if he didn't notice her staring at him. They dined on a delicious array of fruits and cheeses with fresh bread and Greek olives. When her appetite was sated, he was forced to acknowledge her.

"What are you looking at?" he asked.

"You." She tossed a small piece of bread in the direction of a curious squirrel.

"I gathered that. Why?"

She shrugged. "Just trying to figure you out."

"In what way?"

"Well, you refuse to talk about yourself. So, I'm imagining my own scenario of your life story."

He popped the lid on a can of soda and put it on the table in front of her. "What have you come up with?"

She raised her legs onto the bench and wrapped her arms around them. "Let's see. You grew up in a single parent home."

"What makes you think that?"

"You're too guarded to have had the *Leave It To Beaver* family life."

"Brilliant deduction, Sherlock."

"You're a Republican in politics, a loner by choice, and a workaholic by nature."

"An Independent in politics," he corrected.

"But you voted Republican in the last few elections, right?"

"All right. You've got me there. Is that it?"

"No. My guess is that your father is still alive, but you're not real close because he left you. And you're not a big risk taker, at least not where people are concerned."

Nick shrugged. Except for which parent had left, he was surprised how close she was to the truth. Was he some kind of textbook psychology case, or did she really know him better than he thought anyone ever could?

"How am I doing so far?" she queried.

"Close on some points." Falling for Alexis was a major risk. One he swore he'd never take again, though he didn't remember her giving him a choice. "It was my mother who left and my father who raised me."

She rolled her shoulders then stared off into the distance. "That explains a lot."

"What does it explain?"

"Why you don't trust women. Why you've been trying to keep me at a distance."

He arched his eyebrow. "Is that right, Dr. Freud?"

"You tell me."

He had never understood the feminine desire to analyze every situation to death. There was no deep psychology involved. It was pure conditioning. In every relationship, someone leaves. He had spent the last few years of his life making sure he didn't get emotionally involved before the inevitable happened. This time he had ignored the rules.

His gaze traveled slowly over her. The hair, the makeup, the clothes. Her look was cool sophistication, so unlike the warm and wild woman he'd come to know intimately. The changes were only on the surface, he knew, but she had been fighting the changes from the start. She wasn't fighting anymore. Nor would he expect her to.

He thought about the old proverb, "Be careful what you wish for," and understood the truth of those words. The closer she got to his one-time ideal of the perfect woman, the farther away from him she seemed to fade.

Or was he pushing her away?

"We should be getting back to the city." He rose and gave her a hand up.

She draped her arms around his neck. "Don't you want to stick around until after dark and steam up the windows."

He slid his hands over her back and down to her waist. "You are incorrigible."

"I thought my every wish was your command."

"I have to get you home."

She moistened her lips. "Sounds like a plan to me," she whispered against his ear.

Not the same plan he had intended, obviously. Alexis was too irresistible. He would love to take her up on her offer, but why complicate the situation when he knew in his heart he should steer clear.

"You need your rest. The next few weeks are going to be so busy you'll barely have time to breathe."

"All the more reason to enjoy this free time now. Unless you're telling me you're not interested. In which case, I'll . . ."

"Understand," he finished for her.

"No. Call you a liar."

She would be right. Not only was he interested, his emotions were invested. A frightening fact he didn't want to admit. If he couldn't deny the truth, he could delay the inevitable until the campaign was underway and Alexis was sure of what she wanted out of life. He owed her that, and so much more.

Chapter Twelve

Nick leaned over the conference table in the design studio that was covered with photographs of Alexis. The woman could make a career as a model. Not that she ever would. It had been a long week. Unavoidable business had taken him to the West Coast and he missed her more than he ever imagined.

He leafed again through the pictures. She had obviously been busy herself. Three days of shooting at different locations around the city must have been exhausting, but she never revealed it for the camera. Choosing just one shot for the magazine ads was like trying to pick just one thing about Alexis that attracted him. Each different pose caught a different aspect of her personality. Playful, flirtatious, sinful and sweet. He was downright jealous at the range of emotions she had displayed for the photographer.

Yanis entered the room. "What do you think? Is she fantastic or what?"

In more ways than the designer would ever know, Nick thought. "Do you have an idea which one you'd like to go with?"

"That's your area of expertise. Once the graphics are added, which do you think will make the most impact?"

Each and every one had impacted on him. Mostly on his libido, but some had even touched his heart. If he had to pick one, he would choose a photograph that was never intended to be used. A candid shot of her between takes, sitting on white marble steps, in a most undignified manner. A jeweled tiara had tipped to the side of her head and one strap from her blue evening gown had slipped off her shoulder. Her hands were pressed around a Styrofoam cup, as if she was praying to the java gods. This was the epitome of Alexis. All the pretense dropped, she was a harried working girl, taking a coffee break.

"Has Lexie seen them?" Nick asked.

"So it's Lexie, now." Yanis arched his eyebrow and grinned. "She saw them, but I don't think she's objective. She found something wrong with every one. She's so picky."

She strolled into the conference room at that moment. "I'm working with you two. How picky could I be?" As she drew up next to Nick, she deliberately bumped her hip against his thigh. He inhaled a deep, calming breath. If he wasn't feeling enough heat already from studying the photographs, he had to endure what her feminine, fragrant scent did to his hormones.

"Are you finished with Pierre?" Yanis asked.

Nick stepped back and met her gaze. "Who's Pierre?"

"My tutor."

"And what's he teaching you?"

"The art and romance of the French language." Alexis took a small bow that gave him a glimpse of her cleavage. Enough to tempt but not nearly enough to satisfy. *"Bonjour, comment allez vous? Mangez mes shorts."*

"I don't remember that last part from high school language class," Nick said.

"It means *eat my shorts.* I had to learn something useful with all this money you're paying the guy."

"Try not to say that to the French ambassador's son at the gala," Yanis warned her. "You could cause an international incident."

"Why would an ambassador's son be going to a fashion industry gala?"

"You'd be surprised at how many well connected men, including some European dignitaries, have wrangled invitations. All to meet you, Your Highness."

Nick tried to ignore the ache in his gut. It was hard to picture her as royalty when she stood next to him in a pair of cut-offs and a college T-shirt. She *was* a princess, he reminded himself, and there was going to be a parade of wealthy, influential men trying to grab her attention, both at the gala and from that night forward. He had put the eventuality out of his mind the past few weeks.

The future was here. How was he going to make it through the premier? His feelings for Alexis were too deep, too possessive. He would make a scene with the very audience his client was working to impress.

Alexis slipped her hands into her pockets. Nick looked about as at ease with Yanis' announcement as she felt. Did Nick think he had reason to worry? As long as she had him at her side, she wouldn't have eyes for any other man. Especially a bunch of snobs who wouldn't have given her the time of day if they had passed her on the street.

"Cheer up, Lexie," Costas said. "The hardest part is almost over."

For the princess, perhaps, but Alexis got the feeling the hard part was about to begin for her and Nick. The passive way he leafed though the photos on the table showed her just what he thought of the image he had created. Which was fine with her. She wasn't the woman in the picture.

"Are you ready for the final fitting on the taffeta gown?" Yanis asked her.

"I guess so." She laid her hand on Nick's shoulder to capture his distracted attention. "I'll see you upstairs in a few minutes."

She brushed her lips over his mouth. His initial surprise faded fast, and he returned the kiss. At least as passionately as was acceptable with an audience present. As he left the conference room, her eyes remained riveted on his broad shoulders, solid legs and great rear end. The man made an impression coming or going. With an appreciative sigh, she flopped into a chair at the table.

"I think I might be jealous," Yanis muttered humorously.

"Oh, please, you know I'm not your type."

"Princess, you are any man's type. To paraphrase a famous American slogan, you've come a long way baby."

She gazed down at her well-worn shorts. "Even dressed like this?"

"The changes are inside, Lexie. It's your mind-set that's different."

On that point she agreed. She was committed to the project, but she was also committed to her grandmother. Nana was the strongest woman Lexie had ever known. After all the older woman had been through, she deserved to see the family name preserved with regal splendor.

"Let's get to that dress so I can get outta here. I don't want to keep Nick waiting too long."

"You're royalty, darling. You should always keep them waiting."

She was also a woman in love, and she felt as if her time was running out. As if she had gotten stuck in some reverse adventure of Cinderella. Yanis was her fairy godfather and the magic that transformed her into a princess was taking away the man she loved instead of bringing him closer to her.

The next two weeks passed in a whirlwind for Alexis. From sunrise to sunset, her days were filled with wardrobe, makeup and rehearsals. She had seen little of Nick, but she wasn't sure if his absence had been deliberate or work related as he claimed. How could she ask? If she demanded his attention constantly, she would only be feeding his misimpression that she would develop a princess attitude.

Last night she had moved to her suite in the Plaza. As a respectable princess, she needed a chaperone. Marissa was her choice. If Alexis was to get through the next few days, she needed a friend in her corner. She glanced around the beautifully appointed suite. She would trade the lush surroundings for an hour alone with Nick.

"So this is how the other half lives," Marissa said, breaking into her thoughts.

Apparently, her friend was impressed. Alexis smiled. No reason to ruin the experience for her. "Feel free to order room service."

"Did you see the prices on the menu?"

"It's one of your perks as chaperone."

Marissa took a can of Coke and peanuts from the minibar and flopped down in a Windsor chair. "I've always wondered if a bag of five-dollar peanuts tasted better." She tore off the top of the metallic wrapping. "What time is Nick coming?"

"He didn't say." In the past two weeks he hadn't said much of anything concerning the gala. This was the biggest event of his professional career but sometimes he seemed as if he wanted to blow it off.

She knew he was uncomfortable around Princess Alexis. He had created the character to sell a product, but couldn't he see she was still Lexie inside? She looked into the mirror at her meticulously styled hair and perfectly applied makeup. Her appearance might have changed over the past few months, but her feelings for him were not on the surface. It was the one constant that helped her through the upheaval in her life. Nick might think he was doing her a favor by giving her space, but she needed him close by.

Marissa cleared her throat. "I'm eating like a pig and I'm not the one who will be on display tonight. How can you be so calm?"

"Who's calm? I would scarf down the contents of the minibar in a New York minute, but I'd never fit into the dress."

Her gaze traveled to the bed and to the magnificent blue ball gown, an exact duplicate of the coronation dress worn by her great-grandmother over seventy-five years ago. The inspiration had come from photographs that survived the revolution, but Costas had made the design his own. With his own brand of torture. She would have had more breathing room in an old fashion corset.

Being a generous friend, Yanis had offered a

suite for her grandmother, as well as an invitation to the Gala. Nana had declined. Although her strength had nearly returned, she claimed she didn't want to add to Lexie's stress nor take away any attention. Lexie wondered if the memories might be painful as well.

"Is it time to get dressed?" Marissa asked.

Alexis sighed. "I guess so." Out her window, she watched a row of limos line the street, awaiting access to the front entrance. Was Nick in one of them?

She fought the rising anxiety. The night was about to begin. So why did she feel like something was ending?

Nick stood at the far end of the banquet hall and watched the crowd gather around the grand staircase. He hadn't planned on coming tonight. Why watch what might amount to the beginning of the end? Because he had no other choice. He had to be here for her. Alexis was born for this moment, even if she didn't know it. She deserved this. Her grandmother deserved this.

Around the room, champagne flowed from fountains. Waiters clad in tuxedos served Godiva chocolates and caviar to the social elite who had come to the gala. Costas' name alone brought out the cream of society. Add to that one beautiful woman of royal pedigree and the interest grew tenfold.

The din of voices came to a hush when the lights dimmed. Costas stepped to the podium as a spotlight washed over the room.

"Ladies and gentlemen," Costas began. "Thank you for coming this evening. You may have heard the House of Yanis will be launching a new fragrance this fall." He paused through the applause, feigning humility as only he could.

Tension mounted in the room. Or was it only in his body, Nick wondered.

"Yes, well, a great creation can only come from great inspiration," Costas added. Again he hesitated, allowing the anticipation to build. "Allow me to introduce to you, my friend . . . my inspiration . . . Princess Alexis Markova." His hand moved in a theatrical wave toward the marble staircase.

Alexis emerged from the shadows and paused at the top landing. A collective sigh echoed through the cavernous ballroom. A lump caught in Nick's throat, threatening to choke him. She was everything she was supposed to be, everything they had created. Slowly, she descended the stairs with all the poise and grace of true royalty. Her smile was radiant, but had a hint of mystery that left many guests quietly speculating on how they had not met the stunning princess before. There were even a few men claiming they had.

Nick swallowed a groan. Men ogled her, women envied her. He definitely had to leave before he made a scene on her big night. He slipped out the back exit and strode down the nearly empty corridor. Outside the main entrance stood a marquis with the announcement of Royal Blue perfume, pictures of the product, the designer, and of course the spokeswoman. He pulled the photo of Alexis off the marquis. It belonged to the agency. He was not going to leave it as a souvenir for some ambitious fan.

By the time he got to his car, he cursed his temper. He glanced at the photo on the seat. Now that he had taken it, he had to figure out what to do with it. He knew one person who would want the picture. A woman who declined her invitation to the gala so as not to make her granddaughter more nervous.

He drove uptown to the Riverdale apartments. Saturday night traffic made the trip twice as long. By the time he arrived at his destination, he felt no better than when he'd left the Plaza. *What is wrong with me?* he wondered while he rode the elevator to the ninth floor.

The older Markova opened the door. Purse in hand, she appeared to be on her way out. "Nicholas, this is a surprise. Is Lexie with you?" She peeked around his shoulder to check the hallway.

"No, she's still at the gala."

"Then why are you here?"

He offered the photo. "I thought you might like to have this."

She glanced at the photograph lovingly. A proud smile lifted the corners of her mouth, followed ironically, by a sad sigh. "She is beautiful, this princess you've created. But this is not Lexie."

"I know," he said.

"If you know, what are you doing here humoring an old lady? She needs you."

"You wouldn't say that if you saw her to-night."

She pointed to the picture. "She began this for me, but she finished it for you. If you think she doesn't need you, then you're not half as smart as I thought you were."

The older woman had a point. Apparently, love had turned him into an idiot. Alexis had lived up to her contract, even though he knew she would have preferred anonymity to the spotlight. His career was on the line here, not hers.

Nadianna touched his sleeve. "You may escort me to the common room, but then you have somewhere else you should be."

She was throwing him out! He smiled gratefully. With luck, he wouldn't get the same reception from her granddaughter. He glanced at his watch. If he hurried, he could make it back downtown before the gala ended.

Chapter Thirteen

Alexis inhaled a deep, calming breath. She never thought she would be grateful for the hot spotlight, but it had blinded her to the crowds. Her heart pounded in her chest. The worst was over, she told herself. She had made her entrance, smiled brightly for the press, and gushed appropriately over Royal Blue and the House of Yanis. Another hour and she could drop the pretense of a carefree royal princess.

She had met with the long procession of invited guests, but noticeably absent was the one she most wanted to see. Why was she surprised? Nick never made promises. He had gone out of his way to convince her that he was not the man for her. A heavy weight settled over her heart. She usually didn't require a lightning bolt to get a point. Tonight she had been thunderstruck. The gala was a fairy tale, but that didn't guarantee a happy ending.

"Champagne, Your Highness?" Costas offered her a fluted glass.

She smoothed an imaginary wrinkle from the silky taffeta. "No thank you."

He leaned in. To any onlooker, they were two close friends sharing an intimate moment. "What's wrong?"

"He didn't come."

Costas feigned surprise, but she was sure he had noticed too. "He didn't? Well, the traffic is . . ."

Alexis cut off his feeble excuse. "It's not the traffic and you know it. He was here all afternoon for the setup and rehearsal."

"And you let this bother you because . . ." He trailed off, waiting for her to finish.

"You know why."

"You have a room full of men who would happily pay court to you because of your title. You want the one who isn't impressed." Yanis laughed. "You are so much alike, the two of you."

"How so?"

"He wanted you for the campaign precisely because you were not impressed by him or the money."

She shrugged. *"For the campaign*, being the operative words." Evidently, he didn't want her for himself. She arched her back slightly to relieve the coiled tension. "I can't wait for this to end."

"So why wait?"

"The announcement said we're here until ten."

"The champagne flows until ten. You can leave whenever you want." He pressed a brotherly kiss on her cheek. "Cop a royal attitude, Princess. You've earned it."

Costas was right. She had done everything they had asked of her. Until the fall fashion shows, her professional obligations were complete. She needed to go back to where she belonged, if only for the night.

Princess Alexis left the banquet hall under a flurry of photographers' flashbulbs. A half hour later, dressed in her comfortable clothes, Lexie left the hotel unnoticed. The lights of the city sparkled through the limo's skylight as she made her way to Brooklyn with her friend. Some famous writer once said you could never go home. That might be true. But a trip to the old neighborhood might help soothe her broken heart.

Nick alternately cursed himself and Lexie as he crossed the Brooklyn bridge in stop-and-go traffic. After an earful from his client, he'd had to bribe the limo driver to find out where Lexie had gone, although he would have eventually figured it out. She needed to be around friends, and he hadn't been a very good one to her.

Finally, he arrived at the Silver Spur. Weekend cowboys sauntered in and out of the saloon style doors. He entered the smoky bar and gave his eyes a moment to adjust to the muted light. A classic Willie Nelson song wailed from the oversized stereo speakers above Nick's head. He would have preferred to deal with Alexis in the privacy of the hotel room but he had lost that option when he left the Plaza earlier that evening.

His gaze scanned the room until it landed on Lexie. Even in a group of people doing a synchronized line dance, she stood out from the rest. Graceful, sexy and animated, she breathed originality into the repetitive steps. She was flanked all around by men. Anger rose in him. Rationally he had no right to feel this way when he had made no claim to her, but nothing about his feelings had been logical where she was concerned.

Her smile faded when she caught sight of him. She missed a step, but recovered quickly and turned away. Not the reception he was hoping for, but one he deserved. He moved to the bar to wait for the dance to end. Although she still had rhythm, she was obviously self-conscious.

When the music ended, she left the floor from the opposite side of the room. He circled the bar, blocking her path before she could reach her male fan club waiting at a nearby table. Every time he stepped toward her, she backed up, until she was pinned to the wall.

"What do you want?" she asked when he finally cornered her.

"What do you think?"

Her blue eyes sparked with anger. "I think you're worried about your investment. Well, as you can see, I'm fine. I even have my very own designated driver so you don't have to worry. Not that you would."

He clamped his hand over her arm as she attempted to push past him. "Can we talk?"

"Apparently not. Because every time I've tried, you've avoided it." She pulled free and sprinted back to the dance floor as the music started again.

He groaned in frustration. When had he lost control? The moment he'd met her.

He heard a bitter laugh and turned toward the sound.

Marissa's smirk mocked him. "If your expensive gold watch worked, you might have had better luck."

He knew the woman's protective tendencies where her friend was concerned. Any other time, he would have admired the quality. "It works fine."

She slid from her bar stool to glare at him eye-level. "You could have fooled me. Because you were supposed to be somewhere two hours ago."

"I was there. I chose to stay in the background, not that I owe you an explanation."

"No, you don't." Marissa shrugged but her expression softened. "But you do owe her one."

"She doesn't want to listen to me."

"Maybe you're not speaking loud enough."

"Should I start a shouting match in a public place?" he asked.

"If that's what it takes. Although I've always believed that actions speak louder than words."

He couldn't have agreed more. He'd walked out earlier because he hadn't wanted to make a scene. He would not make the same mistake twice.

Lexie threw herself into her dance, hoping the physical exertion would block out her awareness of Nick. Spinning like a top, she lost sense of direction and of where he was in the room. But she was aware of his presence and she was in no emotional shape to deal with him now.

What did he really want? She doubted the country music had attracted him. Or the baby-back spareribs. He certainly didn't want her. He'd made that clear. So why had he shown up in the one place that offered her a mod-icum of peace in the chaos that had become her life?

She spun around and slammed into his solid frame. Instinctively, she grabbed hold of his arms to catch her balance as she struggled for the breath that had been knocked out of her. He felt so good. He smelled so good. She had to get away from him before her mind became as off-balance as her equilibrium.

Strong hands cupped her waist as she tried to pull away. His entrance onto the wooden floor had interrupted the flowing line of dancers behind her and she felt herself being pushed in as many directions as her emotions.

"What are you doing?" she squeaked out.

"What I wanted to do two hours ago when I saw you on that marble staircase." Before his words had time to register, he hauled her over his shoulder like a sack of potatoes. His swift and unexpected action was a crowd-pleaser. Applause and laughter surrounded them, but Nick seemed oblivious. He had to be, because the Nick she knew avoided any public display of emotions.

"Put me down," she growled through clenched teeth.

He ignored her protests and carried her off the dance floor like a Neanderthal might. Heat infused her cheeks. She grasped the fabric of his suit jacket tightly in her hands to keep from sliding off his shoulder.

His words played over in her mind. *What I wanted to do two hours ago when I saw you on that marble staircase.* Warmth replaced the ice that had surrounded her heart. He hadn't missed her opening.

Her last sight before leaving the bar was that of Marissa clapping and waving good-bye. If her friend really thought that these caveman tactics were going to have any effect on Lexie, then Marissa was . . . absolutely right.

If Nick was willing to make a scene, then he must feel something for her. His method was completely out of character and his timing left something to be desired. But the sentiment touched her deep inside.

He continued to storm down the street and around the corner before setting her on her feet in front of his car. With his hands splayed against the roof of the BMW, he pinned her to the cool metal door.

His expression was impossible to read. "So, go on, give it to me."

"Give you what?"

"Tell me I behaved like a jerk."

"Okay. You behaved like a jerk," she said, and then smiled.

He arched an eyebrow in question. "You're not angry?"

"Sure I am. I'm angry that it took you so darned long to do it."

He shook his head as if he couldn't believe her. "Would you have been happier if I had kidnaped you when you were talking to the French ambassador's son and caused an international incident?"

"I would have welcomed it. I had to stand there and smile while he propositioned me." She playfully smacked his arm. "It should have been you."

"I don't want to proposition you. I do have a proposal for you though."

"What kind of proposal?" she asked carefully.

"One I hope you'll want."

She wanted more than maintaining the status quo. She wanted his heart. "Only if it involves you and me as a couple rather than business associates."

"It does."

"Are you sure? Because last time we spoke, you seemed to think I was out of your league. Although how the heck you could think a working girl from Flatbush was out of your league is beyond me."

"Maybe not out of my league, but there were men at the gala who could offer a princess a lot more."

How could he think she needed more? He was all she wanted. She could not have been more obvious or blatant in her desire for him. "I'm not in love with any of them. I'm in love with you."

"That works well, because I'm in love with you too."

"Prove it."

He pulled her into his arms and kissed her soundly, right there on the most crowded street in Brooklyn. It was the kind of kiss that sent her soaring into the clouds. She didn't want it to end. When she came back to earth, she noticed his satisfied grin. "Are you convinced?" he asked.

"I'm not sure. Why don't you take me home and make a believer out of me."

"Your wish is my command."